CHARMING HIS MATE

ALIENS OF OLUURA: BOOK TWO

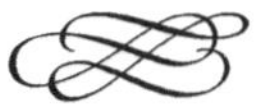

IVY KNOX

Copyright © 2021 by Ivy Knox

This is a work of fiction. Names, characters, organizations, places, events, and incidents are either products of the author's imagination or used fictitiously. Any resemblance to actual persons, living or dead, or actual events is purely coincidental.

All rights reserved. No part of this book may be reproduced in any form or by any electronic or mechanical means, including information storage and retrieval systems, without written permission from the author, except for the use of brief quotations in a book review.

Cover art: Natasha Snow Designs

Edited by: Tina's Editing Services & Mandi's Editing

❀ Created with Vellum

AUTHOR'S NOTE

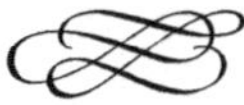

Charming His Mate is book 2 in the *Aliens of Oluura* series. Each book focuses on a new couple and their happily ever after, but reading them in order is way more fun.

Here's book 1:
Saving His Mate: Aliens of Oluura

Content Warning

If you don't have any concerns regarding content and how it may affect you, **feel free to skip ahead to avoid spoilers!**

This book contains scenes that either mention or describe depression, abduction, addiction, as well as substance and verbal abuse which may be triggering for some. If you or someone you know is in need of support, there are places you can go for help. I have listed some resources at the end of this book.

CHAPTER 1

AVA

I watch as Ahlvo's eyelids get heavier, the muscles of his face starting to relax and his lips smacking together as the sedative sets in. His big body twitches slightly on the bed. He lays in his mother Kaiva's med room which is where he's remained, day and night, since returning from Trovilia a little over a week ago.

The crisp night air wafts into the room, leaving a trail of goose bumps down my arms. I tuck Ahlvo's thin blanket around him, carefully avoiding the tender, wounded flesh around the knee of his right leg.

He's about two minutes away from becoming extremely loopy and ten minutes from passing out cold. This has become my favorite time of day—about an hour after the skies turn dark and the sounds of the village grow quiet, when Ahlvo has taken his pain meds to help him sleep.

This is when it's just us. And he's just *him*. He's not stubborn or cranky, or worse—silent and internalizing his pain. He's not trying to sneak out of the med room on his crutch or convince me that his leg is completely healed when it still looks ghastly, and he can't put weight on it.

He's just Ahlvo—the Ahlvo I knew before his leg was busted open by a bullet coated in flesh-eating bacteria. King Muryk, Varrek's dad, was the mastermind behind the horrifying weapon that has caused Ahlvo so much suffering and my many sleepless nights since Ahlvo's return.

I smile at the thought of Ahlvo being the one to kill the king. I try not to wish anyone harm, but that fucker deserved to get his head blown off. In addition to hurting Ahlvo, and attempting to poison Varrek, his own son, he locked women in a dungeon, subjecting them to countless painful experiments to test their fertility. I shudder at how sick the king was. How cruel.

Not that I'm new to the concept of senseless cruelty. I didn't think it could get any worse than the violence and injustice I saw on the news every single day happening to people who looked just like me, but that was before I was kidnapped in the middle of the night and thrown into a glass cage on an alien planet. Turns out space is filled with alien races that commit all kinds of evil acts upon the vulnerable and marginalized.

A loud groan brings me back to the present. "Ayyyye-vah," he slurs. "There you are."

"I'm always here, Ahlvo," I say, giving his wide golden nose a boop.

"Mm-hmm," he mumbles as his unfocused violet eyes scan my face. "That is because you are a ball of squishy moss tucked inside an eternal beam of light. A strong noodle, but also a kind and silly one."

I stifle a laugh. He looks so sincere despite the nonsense that tumbled out of his mouth. "A silly noodle, eh?"

Ahlvo nods proudly. "The silliest, in fact."

"The silliest? You mean you know other silly noodles? Who are they? I want names." I poke his shoulder before checking his vitals on the screen pad next to his bed.

He chuckles, the sound low and husky, and it melts me. It reminds me of the old Ahlvo. The one who carried me out of that dreadful glass cage and brought me here to this idyllic village nestled in the forest of Oluura. The Ahlvo whose main concern in life is making sure his braids are tight and neat. The Ahlvo who cracks jokes at every possible opportunity, and who's so chipper that you wonder if he's for real. I hate that this carefree version of him only awakens when sedatives course through his blood, but until he fully recovers, emotionally and physically, I will cherish these moments.

He shakes his head, suddenly serious. "The other noodles are not silly. They are just noodles. Food to fill our bellies. You are the lone silly one." He reaches for my hand and pulls me toward him. "Come, come. I have a secret I wish to share."

"Ooh, do tell. I love secrets," I reply, leaning down so he can whisper it into my ear.

"Youuu," he drawls in Trovilian, and I'm glad I had the language implantation done in the med tube the other day. Now I can understand the entire clan when they speak their native language, but specifically, Ahlvo's drugged-up babblings. "You glow for me. Light emanates from your skin, from the coiled ends of your mane. I know that others can see it too, but at times, it is as if it comes from your heart. A beacon calling me home."

I stare at him, stunned into silence at his words. I want more than anything to believe those words. That he has never uttered them to another. That he's not telling me this because he's high on pain meds. But I can't accept them as truth. This is Ahlvo. From what I've heard about his past, he's a bit of a playboy. Not only that, but he has never said anything like this to me when sober. He flirts, sure, but he never shares such an open declaration of feelings. Who knows if he'll even remember it when he wakes in the morning?

He lets out a yawn and says, "The ceiling is swirling. Round and round. Do not let it eat you, Aye-vah."

The butterflies that were fluttering in my stomach a moment ago disappear. It's just the drugs then.

"Thanks for the heads up, buddy," I say because that's what we are: buddies. It's a line we established long ago, the day we met, and neither one of us has dared to cross it.

I clean up around Ahlvo's bed, returning extra bandages and healing salves to their assigned shelves. Ahlvo lets out a few more errant groans, and eventually, his light snore fills the room. I turn out the lights and climb onto the med bed next to his.

Despite being a healer-in-training, I'm not required to monitor him overnight, and Kaiva has made it abundantly clear I should go home once Ahlvo's out to get quality sleep in my own bed. But I'm a light sleeper, so whether I'm here or in the little house I share with Chloe and Kate, I wake to the slightest noise. And I'd rather wake to Ahlvo groaning in pain, able to do something about it, than wake up to Kate yelling at a trash can for stealing her lip gloss or something. I don't know; her dreams are crazy weird.

* * *

I wake hours later as sun shines through the massive front windows of the med room. I kick off the tangled blankets and stretch my stiff limbs. Ahlvo's still snoring, and Kaiva is already up, quietly moving around the room, preparing supplies for the day ahead. Her eyes catch mine, and she shakes her head disapprovingly.

"You slept here again, Aye-vah? What have I said about that?" she whispers.

I hop off the med bed and fluff my short curls as I make my way to her side. "I know, I know. I just… wanted to be here. You know?"

"I do, sweet child." She tilts her head and reaches a hand up to softly pat my cheek. "But you will not retain the information you need to become a healer if you are not well-rested. I know that you know this."

Of course, I know this, and she's absolutely right. It's hard to pull myself away from Ahlvo at night though. When I get that glimpse of silly, happy Ahlvo, it feels like I shouldn't move a muscle, and then maybe, if I'm lucky, when I wake up in the morning, everything will be back to normal. Ahlvo will be healed, and our relationship will feel like it did before he was shot. It's a pipe dream. But when things are bleak, you hold onto those little moments that make you smile, grasping at them for dear life.

I yawn, and Kaiva nudges my shoulder. "Go feed yourself, Aye-vah. I will not have you wasting away at my side."

I want to laugh because I've never looked like someone who is "wasting away." I've had several layers of meat on my bones since the moment I entered the world, but Kaiva's classic mom comment puts a smile on my face.

"Okay. I'm going to run home, shower, grab some food, and then I'll be back," I whisper as I make put my boots on by the door.

"Yes, yes. Go," she says while shooing me away with her hands.

I sneak out the front door on tiptoes. Once I'm outside, I book it to my place a few doors down and race inside, kicking off my boots and stripping off layers of clothing as I enter the bathroom. My shower is quick and efficient, and I'm toweling off within four minutes.

After I change outfits in my bedroom, I head back downstairs and run into Kate. Her red hair is a knotted mess, and her feet are heavy as they clomp down the steps.

"Morning, Red. Hungry?" I ask, shoving my feet back into my boots.

"Yeah. Okay," she replies with a yawn.

The moment we get to the food hall, we pile our plates with junasii bread and berries and take our seats at the end of a long table. A soft breeze caresses my skin, and I smile as I squint up at the sun poking through the trees. The day is warm when the wind isn't blowing, and there's a hint of humidity in the air.

"You ready for the wet season?" I ask Kate, who's poking her fork at the berries on her plate like they're beating hearts she's trying to stab.

She doesn't look up, just gives a one-shouldered shrug and says, "I mean, I guess."

After a moment of awkward silence, I ask in a hush, "Wanna talk about it?"

"It?" Kate asks. Her eyes narrow at me as she points her fork in my direction. "Don't get all *shrinky* on me now…"

I lift my hands in surrender. "Girl, I'm trying to help. You don't want to talk? We won't. I just thought I'd offer since you're obviously going through some shit."

She chuckles darkly. "I promise you, Ava, you do not want to be inside my head."

Kate tends to use sarcasm as a defense mechanism to maintain distance between herself and others. Sometimes she forgets how much we went through when it was just the two of us in that disgusting glass cage on Nu'Piix waiting to be auctioned off to the highest alien bidder. Occasionally, I like to remind her that she can't scare me away, no matter how hard she tries.

"Hey, remember that time we lived in a cage and had to share that poop bucket?" I begin, pleased to see her grimace at the memory. I've got her full attention now. "And that time you climbed onto my shoulders to see if you could crack the top corner of the cage with your fist and you missed and we both fell over, hitting the poop bucket, spilling it all over the floor? And since we didn't know what to do, we just started screaming?"

She leans in and looks around to see if any members of the clan are listening. "I thought we agreed to never speak of that again."

I smirk at her and say nothing.

She sighs and finally scoops her deflated berries into her mouth. "It's fine," she mumbles while chewing. "I'm having trouble sleeping, but it's fine. I'm fine. It's nothing, really. It'll be fine."

I watch her rake her fingers through her mussed hair and then rub her eyes. I follow her gaze as it lifts toward the sky and darts anxiously between the treetops. She looks defeated and afraid.

"Look," I say, reaching across the table to grab her pale freckled hand, "if you've changed your mind about staying here, that's okay. Chloe will understand. Now that she and Varrek are mated, I doubt she'll leave with us, but we can keep looking for ways back to Earth."

"No." She shakes her head, pinching her eyes shut. "No. No, I don't want to go back to Earth. I wouldn't have much to go back to anyway. That's not it."

I let out a breath of relief, but I hide it, covering my mouth with my hand. I love it here and would much rather stay than go back to Earth, but if she asked me to go with her, I would.

"It's just…" Kate trails off, trying to find the words. She lets go of my hand and straightens her spine. "You know what? It's fine. I just need to get some rest. That's all. And I will, so don't you worry, Doc."

"Kate, I'm not a doctor. I was in my first year of grad school when I was taken," I remind her.

She digs into her food with fresh enthusiasm and laughs, her mouth full of junasii bread. "Why would you ever want to become a therapist? I can't handle being inside *my* mind, let alone willingly diving into the minds of others."

"Are you actually asking, or are you judging my life choices?" I ask, mentally preparing myself depending on which way she answers.

She finishes her bite and then smiles. "No, I'm really asking. What made you choose that path?"

"Well," I say with a deep inhale, "my dad was a drinker. He was the life of the party and drank socially for as long as I can remember. He drank for happy hour, on business trips, at cookouts on weekends, and at parties at night. It never seemed out of hand, or no more so than any of the people he drank with. But then he started having a nightcap at home after an evening out, or a couple beers with dinner after happy hour, and… Well, it slowly spread from there."

"That's a slippery slope," Kate adds, a flash of recognition in her pale green eyes.

I nod. "My mom didn't seem to mind. Or maybe she was afraid to say something. I don't know. The dynamic they had was that my dad was a pile of problems he refused to address hidden under a nice suit, and my mom was his fixer. She thought if she loved him enough or made his life easy enough, all of his struggles would disappear."

Kate covers her heart with her hand. "Oof, I've known so many women who think like that."

"Right?" I exclaim. "And it makes sense since we're conditioned to believe our duty is to serve. Anyway, my dad's drinking got worse, and then my mom got sick. Breast cancer," I continue, prepared to rush through this part of the story. I hate picturing my mom's frail body in hospice, how she was too weak to talk at the end. "She couldn't prioritize his bullshit anymore because she was busy battling the cancer inside her body. My dad coped by drinking even more and becoming verbally abusive to both of us when things didn't go his way."

My throat suddenly feels dry, so I pause to take a sip of tea.

"My mom died about a year after her diagnosis. I was holding her hand when she slipped away," I say as a familiar combination of sadness and anger fills my chest. "My dad was at home, sleeping off a hangover. She couldn't even depend on him to be there during her last moments."

Kate's eyes are filled with unshed tears, and this time, it's her hand reaching for mine. I look away, blinking furiously so I don't start welling up too. It's been fifteen years, but it's still hard to talk about.

"So to answer your question, I guess I wanted to become a therapist to help people face things before their struggles consume them," I tell her with a jaded smirk.

"Like your dad?" Kate asks.

"No. Fuck him." Then I stop myself, because now I feel like a jerk. "I mean, yes, people *like* him. But, really, I wish my mom had a therapist who told her 'You're not going to be able to fix him. You can want him to face his addiction, but you can't force him into recovery. He needs to fix himself.' Because she deserved better. Maybe if she recognized that earlier, she would've left him and found someone who treated her right. Or maybe she would've left him and been happy on her own. Who knows?"

"Yeah, I get that," Kate says.

"At least she wouldn't have had to clean up after a drunken white guy who wasn't even considerate enough to ask how her day was," I add bitterly. "He came home from work and never asked that question. Not once."

"Is that why you don't want kids? Because of what went down with your dad?" she asks.

I consider this for a moment, even though I've spent plenty of time trying to decide if the two are connected. Sometimes I dig deep into my feelings, checking if there's a repressed memory that has led to my lack of interest in motherhood. Once again, I find nothing.

"No. I keep waiting for the alarm on my biological clock to go off, but it hasn't happened yet," I reply with a shrug.

"Does anyone else here know that you don't want kids?" Kate asks. "Chloe?"

"Um, no. I haven't told her yet."

"You think she'll judge you?"

"I don't think so, but I honestly don't know. She might," I tell her. Choosing not to have children is such a tricky thing to say out loud. If you don't have kids by a certain age, the default assumption is that you can't. And if you clarify that you don't want them, you're seen as selfish or weird. If there's a chance that Chloe will react the same way, I'd rather not take that risk.

Kate and I allow silence to settle between us, and then sigh simultaneously as if we're both cleansing the air of sadness.

"Wanna go see if that asshole dragon left me another decapitated tr'gory on the edge of the forest?" Kate asks, her expression earnest.

I release a laugh from deep within my belly.

"Um, I'll pass, but thanks for the offer," I finally say as the giggles subside. "Why do you think the dragon did that in the first place?"

"I think it might've been a gift for me," she says with a slightly vexed, yet also intrigued, look on her face. "Not that I don't *love* getting headless monsters as gifts, but I mean, at least put it in a box with a bow or something."

I shoot her a smirk, grateful for her ability to lighten the mood with something shockingly gruesome. "Seems reasonable."

CHAPTER 2

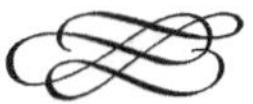

AHLVO

Aye-vah putters around my mother's med room, not noticing my eyes as they follow her movements. She returned from the meal hall several hours ago with her usual dazzling smile despite the weariness in the slump of her shoulders. She is a strong female, this one, but she cannot hide her turmoil from me. My leg wound requires me to be heavily medicated more hours than not, but I know Aye-vah well enough to know that something troubles her.

She returns supplies to their homes upon the shelves, and I try to keep my gaze away from her wide hips as they sway and her full behind as it jiggles with each step. But I fail. This is a failure I embrace, however, because every inch of Aye-vah is glorious, and since I am bed-bound and unable to train with my crew, I refuse to deny myself this gift.

Aye-vah has rarely left my side since I returned from Trovilia. I have allowed my frustration, anger, and sorrow over my injury to control my mind, and she has been witness to all of it. Shame pools in my gut at the thought of her seeing my darkest moments, but when I awaken each day and cannot move the way I used to, when I hear the clashing of sword against sword as my fellow warriors practice without me, I cannot help but sink deeper into this feeling of helplessness.

From this bed, I cannot protect my clan from the bloodthirsty tr'gorys that circle our village at night or the draxilio that flies above us, tormenting Kay-teh's mind. I cannot provide Varrek the support he needs to lead the clan. And if I cannot do those things, what am I but a drain on the clan's limited resources?

I hate this feeling. But no matter how hard I try to keep it hidden, it slips out of me, and always in front of Aye-vah. Generous, brilliant, and radiant Aye-vah. No matter how difficult I am to care for, she remains at my side.

Of course, she remains. It is her duty to care for the injured and sick, says the angry fog inside my head. *She is not here tolerating your stubbornness because it is a delightful experience. She does it because she is determined to become a healer like your mother. It is her calling. She is not here for* you.

The angry fog is a new presence. It is not a voice I heard before I was shot. Despite the grisly sights warriors often encounter on the battlefield, I was never haunted by the ghosts of my enemies. It was an honor to protect my people from those who wished them harm, and I would return from battles long and short with pride in my veins and relief in my heart that I survived. When the virus decimated the people of Trovilia, I would look at my mother and father, still alive somehow, and feel nothing but gratitude that they were spared.

The voice inside my head remained positive and confident. But not anymore.

The moment my eyes cracked open and I found myself in this bed, the angry fog made itself known. It feels red in color, in a way. That is how I picture it when it talks to me. Probably because it makes the back of my neck hot with rage. It floats inside my skull at all times telling me in my own voice that I am a useless lump. That I am nothing if I cannot train with my fellow warriors. That I will never deserve the kindness Aye-vah shows me.

The fog is quite cruel, but is it wrong? I do not know. The longer I am stuck here, the more I believe what it tells me. Surely, once I am able to put weight on both legs and swing a sword with the speed and grace I once had, the fog will disappear. So that is what I must do. I must silence it by proving that I am still the strong fighter I used to be. When the fog is no more, my confidence will return. I know it. My spirit will be healed.

I will be able to resume my quest to woo Aye-vah, my inara, my mate.

She does not know she is my mate, of course. The moment I discovered she was my light, my purpose, my everything, Aye-vah had just stated that she needed a friend. Had I told her the truth of how I felt, I would have scared her away. So I became her friend. And she became mine. I vowed to keep my feelings a secret until she was ready to hear them, until it was clear those feelings were returned.

That moment never came.

Now I am here, stuck in this uncomfortable bed as Aye-vah anticipates my every need, cares for me in every way she can. I lie here and give her nothing in return.

Aye-vah sidles up to me, refills my mug of water, and asks, "I'm heading to the meal hall for lunch. Want me to sneak you some berries?" She gives me a mischievous grin.

This is a little game we have played since she first arrived here on Oluura. Every member of our clan is free to eat as much as they please, especially the b'fiko berries as they grow in abundance on the outskirts of the forest. But Aye-vah would always bring a bowl of berries back to the med room just for me since I had a habit of forgetting to eat between training sessions. When I stopped by during breaks to check on her, tease her, and make her laugh, she would award me with a bowl full of berries and her beautiful smiles.

It was my favorite part of the day.

"Yes, berries sound good, Aye-vah. Thank you," I tell her, trying to conceal my desperation to return to the past.

ONE MOON AGO…

I brush the blood and dirt from my chest as I make my way out of the training grounds and onto the main path of the village. Grotahk walks silently at my side, a hint of amusement on his face.

"Reveling in my defeat, are you?" I tease.

Grotahk's gray eyes widen as they meet mine, almost as if he did not realize I was there at all. "O fah, that is not it, Ahlvo," he says dismissively. "Zohma is leaving the sewing circle for the day. We will be spending the rest of it together. I am looking forward to that."

My mouth hangs open at his words. He is such a quiet, private male. I am shocked he shared so much with me. "You are not returning for training after the midday meal?"

His smile grows wider, a dark golden blush covering his cheeks. "I am not."

We reach the meal hall, and I clap him on the shoulder. "Enjoy your time with your inara, you lucky fool."

Grotahk chuckles at first, but when I remove my hand from his tunic, there is a bloody handprint in its place. He scowls at me. "My Zohma made this tunic for me. You are fortunate I am in such a pleasant mood. Go get cleaned up."

Relief settles my insides, and I laugh off the mess I have made of Grotahk's tunic. "I thank you, old friend."

I grin widely as I head toward the home I share with my family, occupying the floors above the med room.

When I enter my mother's med room, she is showing Aye-vah how to properly apply a bandage around a slender log. Aye-vah looks frustrated that the bandage is not sticking to the bumpy texture of it, and I know what will smooth the furrow in her brow.

"Perhaps you could practice on me, Aye-vah," I tell her with a slight puff to my chest.

Her amber eyes turn hazy as they peruse my arms and legs, but then they widen in horror when they reach my chest. "Good god, what happened to you?" she squeals as she drops the bandage and rushes over to me.

My mother walks over, looking unsurprised by the many cuts on my skin. "Oh, my son. Always the messiest warrior in the bunch."

"Because I fight the hardest," I reply proudly.

"So you were victorious this day?" my mother asks, her eyes narrowed in skepticism.

Aye-vah smirks, adding, "Doesn't look like it."

I cross my arms over my chest and revel in the sight of Aye-vah's pupils growing bigger as they focus on my forearms. "Well, you should see Grotahk. His tunic has blood all over it," I tell them. Not a lie, but not the whole truth—it is that sweet spot where my dignity remains intact.

My mother crosses the room and grabs a fresh roll of bandages. "No matter. This shall be a good exercise for you, Aye-vah. Instead of wrapping the log, you may clean and dress Ahlvo's wounds."

"Oh, um, are you sure I'm ready for that, Kaiva?" Aye-vah asks as she bites her luscious lip nervously.

"I am certain you are ready," she says as she heads for the front door. "I will be at the meal hall. Good luck on your first patient."

I hop onto the first med bed in the treatment area and lie down. "Heal me, Aye-vah. I am in dire need of your assistance," I say with a wink.

Her nerves visibly dissipate as a smile lights up her face. "Oh, I'm sure you are, Casanova."

I scratch my head, puzzled. "What is this word?"

"It means you're a shameless flirt."

Her soft brown hands work swiftly, expertly, as she gathers the wound care supplies and places them on the tray next to the bed. It is then that I realize Aye-vah does not lack expertise when it comes to wound care, only confidence. As long as I keep her mind elsewhere, perhaps she will not be held back by her nerves. I decide to continue distracting her with my charms... solely for her benefit, of course.

"You think I am a flirt?" I ask.

"Buddy, I know you're a flirt," she replies as she wipes the dirt and dried blood from my chest with a clean wet rag. "All you have to do is

flex your bicep or flash those fangs and females fall all over them-selves. I've heard the stories."

Stories? I suppose I have accrued a long list of former pleasure mates. Does that bother Aye-vah? Is she jealous? My insides flip at the thought. But her reaction to hearing these "stories" does not appear to contain the fury of someone who is jealous. Rather, it seems she is amused by this reputation of mine, and maybe, slightly disgusted as well.

I brush this information aside and lean into the image she has of me, if just for a moment. I flex my bicep and shoot her a wide toothy grin. "I do not see you falling, Aye-vah. Are you somehow immune to my beauty?"

She shakes her head and releases a loud chuckle. The sound is wild, uninhibited, and it goes straight to my cock. If only Aye-vah knew how much power she holds over me. How the faces of past pleasure mates have blurred to nothing since the moment we met. How it feels as if I did not fully exist until she stepped into my life.

"I'm not blind, Ahlvo," Aye-vah says as she applies the healing salve to my cuts. "I think I know you too well. I know you're always just messing around, looking for a reaction. It's a fun game."

A game.

How could my inara think the attention I have showered her with is part of a game?

And then I remember: it is because I am her friend. Her buddy. It is what she needs, and I am honored to fulfill that need. Although I am quite certain I can someday win her heart, what if all she ever wants from me is friendship? Am I comfortable with that?

"Yes," the voice inside my head says instantly. "So long as Aye-vah is near, and you are able to protect her, that is enough."

My cock twitches against the waistband of my leggings as if to reply, "Is that truly enough for you? Because it is not for me." But I ignore it because Aye-vah's needs will always surpass my own.

"Yikes, you're all kinds of beat up, aren't you?" she mutters.

I look down at the array of cuts across my chest and shrug. "Today we trained with daggers. This," I gesture to my chest, "was unavoidable."

Aye-vah starts cutting the bandages into strips and pauses while looking thoughtfully at the sterile medical blade in her hand. "I suppose I need to learn how to defend myself at some point. Chloe is learning how to throw knives with Varrek, and I have to admit, I'm a little jealous."

Jealous? This is a wish I can easily grant her.

"I can teach you how to wield any weapon you choose. I am the most-skilled warrior in our crew. Who better to teach you?" I boast.

She scrunches her nose, a facial expression I find so appealing that I could spit. "Wait, you're the best warrior? I thought that was Varrek, since, you know, he's the leader."

"He is a supremely skilled warrior, this is true. And he is the best leader. That combination is why he is the head of our crew and our clan. I do not wish to lead... only fight," I say, wiggling my brows.

She starts covering my lacerations one by one with bandages, remaining quiet while she works. Eventually, she says, "Eh, one thing at a time. I need to focus on mastering this whole healer thing first." Then she locks her eyes onto mine. "You'll protect me in the meantime, right?"

I take her hand and place it over my heart. "Always, Aye-vah. I shall always protect you."

Her big brown eyes search mine. What is she looking for? I wonder as I lift my head slightly off the bed, closer to hers.

She leans in too, a move so subtle I almost did not notice it. The distance starts to close between us as her gaze drops to my mouth. Instinctively, I glide my tongue over my fangs and then my lips to wet them. Her eyes follow the movement, and I hear her suck in a breath.

Her scent, sweet like honey and citrus, fills my nose. I breathe it in, letting it occupy my lungs completely. I never want to smell anything but her. Aye-vah folds her bottom lip under her blunt teeth and bites into the thickest part, causing me to tighten my grip on her hand over my heart. I can feel my cock throb beneath my pants, the fabric tightening.

I do not move. I do not breathe. I fear that either of these things will break our trance. We shift closer, my neck straining as I lift my head to meet her, as she bends down to meet me. Her face relaxes and her eyes soften as if she has given herself permission to let this happen.

My heart to beats faster, louder. Perhaps, she does return my feelings. Perhaps, she would enjoy spending her life by my side. Perhaps, this is precisely what she wants.

I reach my other hand up to cup her jaw and bring her lips to meet my own...

A loud crash makes us jump. We pull away from each other, jerking in the direction of the noise.

The log.

It has fallen off the steel table and now lies on the floor with a strip of bandages loosely wrapped around it.

Aye-vah covers her face with her hand and shakes her head in displeasure.

Does she regret what almost occurred? I pray to the goddess she does not.

I shoot the log a murderous glance for its rude interruption, silently wishing I could avenge the moment we lost by destroying the log's entire family. But that would require me to desecrate the land on which we live, and that is something our clan does not do.

Aye-vah straightens and pinches her eyes closed. When she opens them again, she is not the Aye-vah I almost kissed. Her gaze is serious. She is Aye-vah the Healer, and I am her patient. Her friend. "Okay, so I think you're all set here. Your cuts are bandaged up and should heal within a few days." She rushes away, nodding rapidly.

I clear my throat and sit up on the med bed. "I thank you, Aye-vah."

She smiles nervously, and holds up a finger. "I almost forgot..." she says as she runs over to the steel table lining the far wall and grabs something on the shelf beneath it. She races back to me with her hands behind her back and a sneaky grin on her face. "Snuck you some berries from breakfast. I know you probably haven't eaten much today." Her expression is sheepish but excited.

"Why, you little thief. What will the clan say when they discover one of the humans is hoarding berries?" I say with a chuckle. I pop one into my mouth and groan as it explodes under my fang. "My favorite."

"I know, buddy," Aye-vah says quietly.

In an effort to forget how close I came to tasting my sweet Aye-vah, I toss my head back and dump the rest of the berries into my mouth at once. Aye-vah begins cleaning up her supplies on the tray next to me, and it is clear that she is eager to get back to work. I decide to let her be and place the empty bowl on the steel table where the log sat earlier, then pick up the log as I head toward the door.

Once outside, I pass my mother as she returns from the meal hall. She watches as I stride toward the training grounds. Finally she stops, turning toward me, her brow bunched in confusion as her eyes stray to the bandaged log in my grip. "What are you doing with that?" she asks.

I do not bother turning to face her. I simply holler over my shoulder, "Revenge."

CHAPTER 3

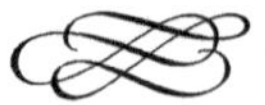

AVA

After inhaling a small plate of bread and meat for lunch, I fill a bowl with Ahlvo's favorite berries and rush back to the med room just in time for his diagnostic check inside the med tube.

As much as Ahlvo hates being inside the cramped glass cylinder, I know he's eager to learn how much his wound has healed in the week since we last scanned it. Since it's a flesh wound, it's easy to tell with the naked eye how it's healing, but the med tube takes it a step further, looking at the tissue beneath the surface so we can get ahead of any infections or decay.

Rain patters against the glass windows of the med room. Apparently, the wet season has begun.

I place the bowl of berries on the tray next to his bed and move to stand with Kaiva as the tube beeps and whirs. I pick at my cuticles, nervous for the results. My breath hitches as the screen pad in Kaiva's hands blinks with the final diagnostic report. Since it's in Trovilian and I can't decipher any of it, I zero in on her face as she reads it, desperately hoping the results are good. Ahlvo's mental state is fragile at the moment, and I'm not sure how he'll handle more setbacks. I hate seeing him frustrated.

The glass top of the med tube lifts with a *whoosh*, and I reach inside to guide Ahlvo out. He's over seven feet tall and as wide as a train, so while I can't support his full weight, I'll take some of the burden. Regardless, he leans heavily on the crutch under one arm as he gently drapes his other arm across my back and hops out. Even now, he's worried more about me than himself, and the evidence makes my heart jump inside my chest.

I guide him to his bed, and he plops down with an exasperated sigh. "Well?" he asks Kaiva.

She puts down the screen pad and closely examines the angry-looking flesh that covers the better part of Ahlvo's leg. The wound is still leaking pus, and the edges of the surgical site are lined with dried blood and puffy blisters. The skin surrounding the wound has the uneven and pink appearance of a burn, and imagining the pain makes me wince. We clean it every two days, allowing the healing salve to do its job, but it's still not quick enough for Ahlvo.

"It is not where we want it to be, but nonetheless, it has improved since last week," she says, reaching for the salve and fresh bandages.

Ahlvo throws his head back on the bed in a huff. "What can we do? There must be something we can do. I have never had an injury that took this long to heal."

"You have never had an injury like this one, my son," Kaiva replies softly. "We are giving you all the medicines your body requires. The only thing you need is time." She holds his face in her hands. "The med tube cannot accelerate your healing. It can only tell us what is happening and perform necessary procedures. But there is no procedure needed here. Give yourself time to heal, Ahlvo. I beg of you."

My lip trembles as I watch them, and I think of my mother, so kind and gentle, much like Kaiva. I miss her terribly, especially when I'm sleep-deprived and stressed. She always made everything better, easier, less scary.

"I cannot help the clan from this wretched bed!" Ahlvo yells as he slams his fist on the tray. The bowl of berries goes flying and they scatter all over the floor. Then he throws his pillow across the room, his tone full of outrage and self-loathing as he shouts, "I am nothing here!"

"Knock, knock," Chloe says in her usual chipper tone as she enters, and I'm so relieved by the interruption that I rush over to her with my arms outstretched.

"Hey, you," Chloe whispers as she rubs my back. "Everything okay?"

I release her and plaster on a smile for her and Varrek. Varrek stands closely behind Chloe, giving me a similarly concerned glance.

"Yep. All good here," I lie. "Everything okay with you guys?"

Varrek reaches for Chloe's arm and points her bloody elbow in my direction.

"Cloh-ee tripped on the stairs of our home and is now wounded. Please heal her. I cannot take this," he says, his voice pained.

Chloe gently pulls her arm from Varrek's grasp and pats his side. "Really, I'm fine. It's just a scrape. No big deal."

It's not a surprise he's reacting this way to a minor scrape. He's been obsessed with Chloe since the moment he first saw her, and I often wonder how he gets anything done with that much love consuming his heart. It's clear that she loves him too, but Varrek is... a lot. He stomps around like his past traumas live in his feet and he's punishing the ground for everything he's ever lost. It freaked me out at first, but now that I've gotten to know him, I understand that he's an intense, brooding dude with a lot on his plate. He also worships Chloe, so that's enough for me.

Kaiva smiles at Chloe and Varrek as she retrieves Ahlvo's pillow and asks, "Aye-vah, can you take care of Cloh-ee's wound for me?"

"Certainly," I tell her. "Right this way." I lead my bestie to the bed farthest from Ahlvo to give everyone a little extra privacy. She takes a seat and rolls up her sleeve.

I grab some water, cleaning rags, bandages, and salve and place them on the tray next to Chloe's bed. I get to work cleaning her elbow as Varrek quietly excuses himself to check on Ahlvo.

"So how's mated life?" I ask. "Is it weird having him inside your head twenty-four seven?"

Chloe dips her chin, her cheeks turning cotton-candy pink. "No, it's not like I imagined at all. It's like we're together all the time. Like he's right next to me even when he's not," she mutters. Chloe smiles and spaces out for a little too long, and I assume she's talking to Varrek through their mental bond. "I love it," she finally says.

I try to picture what that would be like, to have someone in my head constantly. I'm not sure I'd enjoy it. What about all the time I spend pondering different *Star Wars* fan theories? Or when I imagine which of my favorite philosophers would win in a thumb war—Kant or Kierkegaard? Sometimes I try to mentally recount my entire day in Latin, just to see how much I remember from school. These are happy places for my mind. Would my mate judge me if he heard them? Would he think I was odd? Or too much of a nerd?

"I'm glad," I tell her as I apply the salve to her elbow. "You deserve all the good things."

Her eyes narrow at my words. "And what about you?"

"What about me?" I say with a shrug.

"Ava, you look like you haven't slept in weeks. Your hands are shaking." She waves her hand an inch from my nose in an attempt to gain my full attention. "Talk to me. Do you need a break from watching Ahlvo? I told you, Varrek and I don't mind taking some night shifts so you can get some sleep. You need it."

I put the finishing touches on her bandaged elbow, and my eyes meet hers. I want to argue, but I can't. The truth is I haven't slept more than an hour at a time since Ahlvo came back from Trovilia. And even before then, while he was gone, I wasn't sleeping because I worried he might not come back at all. I do need sleep. But that would require me to be away from Ahlvo at night, and nighttime is when Ahlvo is his old self.

I suppose I could always leave after he gets silly and passes out, but sometimes he has nightmares, waking up scared and confused. When that happens, he seems relieved the moment he sees my face. Would he have the same reaction if Varrek or Chloe were here instead?

Besides, it genuinely feels like he needs me, and I like being needed by him. There will come a day when he can walk again, when he won't be stuck in that bed. He'll go back to the old Ahlvo—happy and carefree—and we'll be closer because of the time we're spending together now. I can do this.

"Really, I'm fine, Chlo," I promise her. "It's tough right now because Ahlvo is in a funk, and I hate seeing him like that. But his leg is healing." I let out a deep sigh. "Just gotta stick it out until we're on the other side."

She blows a hair out of her eyes, and her mouth forms a grim line. Clearly that was not the answer she wanted. "If you say so."

"Besides, I'm learning a lot right now: how to place an IV, what the different salves do, et cetera. I promise I'll let you know if I need help."

I clean up the supplies from her tray and return to stand at her side.

"We need to talk about Kate," she says, her tone somber.

"Yeah, I had breakfast with her this morning, and she seemed completely out of it."

Chloe nods. "It's gotten really bad. I don't even know what to do anymore. Maybe you could talk to her? Flex that old therapist muscle for a bit?"

"I was never a therapist. I was in school to become one. Big difference."

"But you have *some* knowledge. More than the rest of us, anyway," she pleads.

"I tried to talk to her at breakfast. It didn't work."

Chloe's chin dips, her gaze dropping to the floor. "Well, maybe you could try again. At our place? Maybe Kate would open up in private, you know, not surrounded by people at the meal hall."

I want to say no. That I'm being pulled in too many directions right now and don't have it in me to take this on. But it's Kate, my cage buddy. We shared so much in there: nightmares, piles of kibble, panic attacks, memories of our old lives—we even created a secret language at one point, including a password to use if we ever got into a jam and needed to tell the other person we were in danger without actually saying it. It was "bologna foot."

I chuckle quietly at the memory. I tried telling her that we can just say "danger" instead of a nonsense phrase, but Kate insisted that "bologna foot" would be better, or at the very least, more fun.

"Okay, I'll do it. I'll talk to her tonight," I tell Chloe. As exhausted as I am, I can't rest peacefully knowing Kate is struggling.

Chloe's big eyes brighten. "Yay! Thank you," she squeals, pulling me in for a tight hug. Then she whispers, "See how easy that was—asking for help?"

I pull back to look at her, rolling my eyes but smiling. "Fine. You're right. If Varrek can keep an eye on Ahlvo tonight, that would be a massive help. I'll stick around for Ahlvo's loopy time, and then once he passes out, I'll head back to our place to be with Kate."

"Yes!" Chloe exclaims, clapping her hands together triumphantly. "He will absolutely stay here tonight."

"Hey, has Varrek mentioned any dragon sightings since the last one? Or *draxilio* or whatever they call it?" I ask, changing subjects.

"The one with the headless tr'gory? No. But he still has the crew doing daily patrols." Chloe says, and then pauses, looking nervous. "Why? Did Kate mention a new one?"

"No," I reply. "Look, I believe her. I know she's not making it up."

"Me too!" she insists.

"So since this dragon is real and flying over the village pretty consistently, are we really safe here?"

Chloe jerks back, looking shocked. "Of course, we are. The clan has lived here for over four years, and this is the first time there's been a dragon issue."

A dragon issue.

I try to be open-minded, and I think I've adapted pretty well to the fact that I can never return to my home planet and now plan to live among a clan of golden aliens for the rest of my days. But dragons? I'm not on board with dragons. I am not comfortable knowing they truly exist, live close by, and can scorch our entire village in a single fiery breath.

"That's true," I reply, attempting to be optimistic like Chloe. "Since it hasn't happened yet, it probably won't."

She looks out the window, clearly nervous. I've scared her. Shit.

"Hey, don't listen to me," I reassure her. "I'm exhausted and stressed. I'm spinning out a bit."

"This does not seem wise," Varrek says from across the room, and my head swivels immediately in their direction. In Varrek's hand is a mug of ale with a closed lid on top.

The mug is about three-quarters full, and as Ahlvo realizes I'm watching, his expression shifts, like a puppy sitting next to a chewed-up shoe.

I storm over and grab the mug from Varrek's hand. "Is this yours?" I ask Ahlvo.

Kaiva and Chloe join us, and now everyone is focused on Ahlvo, waiting for his response.

Finally, he says, "Uh, yes. It is mine."

"What the hell, Ahlvo? We've talked about this."

Kaiva and I have told Ahlvo that he cannot drink alcohol while on the sleep medication we give him. This is the second time we've taken ale away from him. It can be dangerous. Realistically, it would take a lot of booze (or ridiculously strong booze) to become a serious health risk to someone Ahlvo's size, but still. We've been focused on eliminating alcohol as a potential coping mechanism for him.

Besides, watching someone I care about use alcohol as a crutch is a serious red flag. I can't do that again. I might be Ahlvo's healer, but I am *not* his fixer.

Ahlvo's eyes dip down in shame, and he mutters something under his breath about helping him "ignore the fog," followed by a quiet apology.

I take the mug outside and dump the ale onto the blue moss-covered ground. I drop the mug in the dirty dish tub and start angrily folding the clean rags. Chloe comes over and stands next to me, silently, but I don't look up. I'm too pissed. My hands shake as I attempt to swallow my frustration.

It's a good thing I'm not Ahlvo's mate, because this is too similar to my dad, and I refuse to watch as he slides into a life of addiction and self-loathing. He's my friend, though, so I do want to help him.

Can I even do that? Ignore the attraction I feel for Ahlvo while giving him the tools to help him climb out of this hole? I have to be careful not to take on his emotional struggles as my own. I have to maintain that distance. He's not mine to save—he has to want to save himself. That's the only way he'll get through this.

"Looking forward to your night off?" Chloe finally asks.

I drop the cloth in my hands and pinch my eyes shut, fighting back the flashing memories of my dad. "More than you know," I whisper.

CHAPTER 4

AVA

As I sit next to a highly sedated Ahlvo, the door to the med room opens a crack, and the darkness of night floods in. Both Kaiva and Rumo turn their heads toward the entrance too. Then I see Varrek's emerald eyes peeking in as they search for mine. I wave him in but put a finger to my lips indicating he needs to be quiet.

He nods, gingerly stepping inside and toeing off his muddy boots. He shakes the light trickle of rain out of his silver strands and shuffles toward me. Ahlvo's on the verge of being completely conked out but still hovering in a light snooze.

I tuck his blankets around his body, and after a few minutes of watching his breaths get shallow and quiet, I turn to Kaiva. "Okay, he's out. Hopefully that extra sedative will keep him out until I'm back in the morning."

"Do not worry, Aye-vah," Varrek reassures me. "I will keep a watchful eye on Ahlvo while you are gone. He shall be fine."

I exhale deeply. Even though I initially resisted the idea of leaving Ahlvo for the night to spend time with Kate, I'm really excited for girl time and to sleep in my own bed. I've missed my bed. I've missed the girls. I've missed our cute little house.

This will be a good night, I decide.

"You have taken such great care of my son, Aye-vah. I do not know how to thank you," Rumo says, giving my shoulder a light pat.

Rumo isn't around very often as he's usually off on a hunting trip, but when he is, he's constantly joking around and lightening the mood. I adore him. Ahlvo is very much his father's son, but tonight, his words are serious and sincere. I think he knows how hard it's been for me to see Ahlvo in such a dark place. I assume that it's hard on him too.

"You know… just doing my job," I say with a dismissive smile.

"No, you are not," Rumo replies. "This is beyond your duties as a healer, and I think you know that too." He gives me a wink like he knows my secret and vows to keep it. Then walking over to Kaiva, he presses his lips to her hand and guides her upstairs for the night, both of them giving Varrek and me a small wave as they ascend.

"Go on," Varrek says. "Kay-teh needs you."

"Okay. Thanks for covering," I whisper as I open the door.

He gives me a subtle nod and takes a seat at the foot of Ahlvo's bed.

I jog down the main path, the rain has finally paused, and elation fills my bones as I reach our house. But before I open the door, movement catches my eye.

It's Kate emerging from the bushes. Her hair is in loose pigtail braids that are damp from the earlier rain. Her long-sleeved shirt is tied in a knot at her waist, the sleeves bunched at her elbows. She's coming from the same direction of her dragon sightings, and as tempted as I am to scold her for being in the forest after dark, I know that kind of response will only result in defensiveness, so I tread carefully.

"Hey there, Red," I say. "Whatcha doing in the forest at this time of night? Collecting acorns?"

"Technically, this whole village is 'in the forest' so I could ask you the same thing," she says, her mouth curling up on one side.

"Don't sass me, girl," I tease. "You know what I'm saying."

She sighs in a dramatic fashion, not unlike a teenage girl who was just told to put her phone down at the dinner table, and kicks at a clump of moss under her boot.

Deflection and avoidance—these are the bricks in her emotional wall. And tonight, I plan on using my very limited training to help her break it down and get to the root of what's caused her so much stress lately. If that doesn't work, my plan B is to let her vent.

"Come on, Kate. Do you really want us to think of you as 'that girl who got swallowed whole by a tr'gory'?" I ask, knowing dark humor is the clearest path to her heart.

She chuckles like I knew she would. "I just needed some fresh air. I… wasn't ready to fall asleep."

"You dreaming about her again?"

"No, I wish. I mean, I am having dreams, just not about her," Kate replies, her tone flat.

Kate has always had vivid dreams. Sometimes they're so intense that she talks or yells during them. And she always remembers them the next day. If I have a dream I remember, which is rare, I'll forget it by breakfast. But Kate remembers them all.

It's the reason she's felt like an outcast her entire life. Not only are her dreams intense, they also feature a reoccurring character she's never actually met: her great-aunt Milly. Kate told her parents about the dreams when they started, but they accused her of making it up, so she kept them to herself from that day on. At least, until she met me.

"I miss her," Kate says with a sad smile. "Did I ever tell you how Grammy Ruth was convinced Auntie Milly was a witch?"

"What? No, but I'm gonna need those deets immediately, please."

"Apparently, that's why me and my brothers were never allowed to see her," Kate says. "Pretty sure she was just a bra-burning feminist who didn't want a husband or kids. I don't think she actually dabbled in the dark arts."

"I thought women were only accused of witchcraft for being husband-less in like the seventeenth century."

Kate rocks back on her heels and nods. "Yeah, Grammy Ruth took old-school thinking to the extreme."

"But that just speaks to the incomparable radness of Great-aunt Milly. Anytime you're ruffling the feathers of close-minded folks, you're living right," I tell her.

"This is true," Kate agrees.

Since the night Kate was kidnapped from Earth, Milly has been absent from her dreams. It's one of the things that troubles Kate. Clearly, though, it's not the only thing.

"So what are these new dreams about?" I ask, trying to lead her toward the door to our house, but Kate's feet remain planted a few feet away. "What? You don't want to go in?"

Kate says nothing, but her mouth twitches.

"Ah, Chloe doesn't know about any of this?" I ask.

Kate nods, and then her cheeks blush a bright pink. "It's not that I don't trust her, it's just… she treats me like family, and I don't want that to change."

I sigh and pull Kate in for a hug. She stiffens at first, like always, but eventually her arms wrap around my back and she sags against me. She feels so isolated here and I hate it. From what she's told me about her childhood, there's never been a time when she felt accepted. "Don't worry. It'll just be you and me tonight."

I pull her inside, and we find Chloe in the kitchen area, filling a mug with water.

"Hey, babes!" she says, her bright smile lighting up her heart-shaped face.

I'm not at all worried about Chloe trying to turn this into a girls' night. She asked me to speak to Kate alone and was thrilled when I agreed to it.

Almost on cue, Chloe lets out a massive and clearly fake yawn. "I'd love to stay up and hang, but I am beat," she says.

She pulls us together for a quick squeeze. "Sleep well, ladies," she says before heading up the stairs to her room on the top floor.

Kate and I kick off our boots by the door, fill our mugs with water, and head up to her room on the second floor. We crawl into her bed and lean against the wall as we sip from our mugs.

"So…" I start, "what are these new dreams about?"

Kate takes a deep breath in and then out. "Um, well? A guy, actually."

That I was not expecting.

"Is that so? Bruvix?" I ask, teasing her.

"What?! No. Not Bruvix," Kate replies instantly.

I've seen the way Bruvix looks at her and the way he talks to her. He's a surly, intimidating guy covered in gnarly scars, but with Kate, he's a bit softer. "There's nothing there?"

"No, not at all," she says with certainty. "Sometimes I'll catch him following me like the Hexrins do occasionally, and when I call him out on it, he gets cranky. He's like a brother more than anything."

"Wait, the Hexrins have been following you?"

"Yeah…" she says with a narrowed gaze. "I assumed you or Chloe or Varrek asked them to make sure I wasn't going outside the forest."

Huh. That's bizarre. "Uh, no. Nobody asked them to follow you."

She shrugs with a sigh as if too exhausted to care.

I decide to circle back to that later. I don't hate the idea of the clan pitching in to care for Kate, but following her through the village seems creepy.

"Who have you been dreaming about then?" I ask. A gust of air blows through her open window, and we tug the blankets up to our chins.

"I don't know who he is. I've never seen him outside of my dreams. But now, every time I fall asleep, he's there." Her voice grows distant as she recalls this mysterious dream guy. "Sometimes he's with me as I revisit events from my past, but then there are times when it feels like I'm a guest in his memories."

"Hmm. How do you feel in the dreams when he shows up?"

Kate's pale cheeks turn bright pink as she looks down at the blanket. "I feel safer. It's like he's there to protect me, even when he's reliving his own pain."

I think about that for a moment—about how comforting it would feel to be inside of a nightmare, especially one you've lived, and to have someone there to protect you. If I had a dream guardian like the one she describes, I'd love going to sleep. So why does she seem like she hasn't slept in days?

"Tell me more about him. Is there something about this dream guy that makes you uncomfortable?" I ask.

She pinches her eyes closed and hugs her knees to her chest beneath the blanket. "Yes. In the dreams, I want to trust him, but I don't think I should."

"Why not?"

"Because he keeps telling me to leave the village."

I keep my face neutral despite the sudden stiffness in my shoulders. I've never been big on dream analysis as a method of self-reflection—I've always assumed dreams are a compilation of random images that cycle through the brain during sleep, nothing more—but Kate's dreams are hard to dismiss. And since she's feeling like an outcast among the clan, I'm not at all surprised that this "dream guy" is telling her to leave. I think it's her subconscious reinforcing the idea that she doesn't belong here.

I am relieved, however, that she doubts him, like she doesn't actually want to leave the village, because that would put her in danger. She'd be out of the protective cover of the forest and exposed to that blue dragon that seems to be hunting her, as well as the tr'gorys and other predatory creatures lurking outside the forest.

There's also part of me that thinks all of these elements are connected, and what she needs right now is to feel a sense of community, not continued isolation.

"I think you're right not to trust him," I tell Kate. "Leaving the village would be a bad idea, obviously. Chloe and I are here for you."

"Yeah, I know that," she mutters with a sigh. "I'm just sick of feeling like this."

"I know," I say as I put an arm around her.

Eventually, Kate shifts the conversation to lighter topics. We talk about Nalba's current lineup of strange inventions and that delectable sauce Waldric made for Maevstra. We complain about the wet season and laugh about Waldric's obvious crush on Nalba.

As our eyes grow heavy, I'm too lazy to go upstairs to my bed. Kate tells me to stay put and so I do. I yank the covers over my head and pass out within moments of hearing Kate's steady breaths.

Hours later, a guttural scream yanks me from a deep sleep. "Ahl-vo," I whisper.

CHAPTER 5

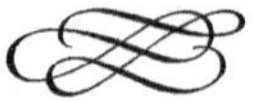

AHLVO

My eyes shoot open, my body filled with nervous energy. I am late for… something. Training? It is possible. Did Varrek entrust me to lead the session today? Yes, yes, that must be it. He is probably busy with his new mate and needs me to take over.

I sit up too quickly, and a sharp pain flares behind my eyes. I rub my eyelids and massage my temples, willing the pain away.

There is no time for this, I think to myself. I must hurry to the training grounds.

My vision is slightly blurred, which confuses me. But no matter, I am perfectly capable of leading our crew in today's training session. Whatever clouds my mind, I can push through it.

The sun has not risen yet which explains why the room is so dark.

I tug the covers off my body and hurl my legs off the bed. But the moment my right heel hits the floor, a groan escapes my lips. I look down at my leg, and my stomach sinks as I realize my leg is still injured. But Varrek is depending on me, so I must not let him down. I grab my crutch and hop to the door.

I reach for the handle and miss. When I try again, I see that there are two door handles. When did that happen? Why would my mother install a second door handle? What is this madness? I shake my head and pinch my eyes shut for a moment. When I look again, there is only one.

A sigh of relief whooshes out of me.

Okay, so my eyes are not as sharp as usual. That is fine. I shall adapt.

We will practice with something other than daggers or swords today. Maybe bows and arrows. It is much less dangerous if I see two targets in the distance than engage in hand-to-hand combat with sharp objects.

I bound outside and welcome the crisp air that brushes my skin. I lean on my crutch and smile because I am no longer trapped in that bed. My injury is no longer prohibiting me from doing my duty, from protecting the clan. I am healed. Well, not healed, but healed enough for Varrek to let me train again. Why else would he ask me to take over for him?

Exhilaration hums throughout my body. It is a familiar feeling, a feeling I have missed while being bedridden. It is the rush of adrenaline signaling that my warrior instincts are about to take over, allowing my finely honed battle skills to guide each movement. With a weapon in my hand, I am home. My soul is at peace.

I hobble toward the training grounds, the clearing softly illuminated by the growing light of morning. My gaze locks on that sacred space as I move toward it. It is then that I notice a large swinging tail as it swipes through the dirt, the single spike at the end leaving a trail behind it. I stop in my tracks, watching, waiting…

Finally, the large creature steps into the center of the training grounds, smoke puffing out of its large blue muzzle.

Blue. The creature is blue.

Is this… the draxilio? The one that has been taunting Kay-teh? The beast that has been circling *my* village, spreading fear among *my* clan? This predator thinks it can stomp around our training grounds whenever it chooses? The land where the elite warriors of Trovilia practice hand-to-hand combat each day so we can protect our clan and our home?

No. No, I will not allow this.

I shuffle forward, staying as quiet as I can with my crutch, my eyes fixated on the draxilio. It blurs occasionally, but I will not let that deter me. I can defeat this intruder.

My claws extend, and I can feel the familiar surge of rage in my veins. I am known in battle for my ruthlessness, and in this moment, I feel that peace. Saliva fills my mouth as I envision tearing its throat out with my fangs.

I pat my stomach and waist, realizing I am unarmed. It is no matter. If I circle around the training grounds to the weapon hut, I can pull something from there. My clan is fast asleep, but I can do this on my own. And when the sun lifts high into the sky, the clan will discover that poor, wounded Ahlvo has destroyed the draxilio, that he did it all on his own. Varrek will see and know in his heart that he can rely on me. I can protect my people.

The massive blue draxilio lumbers around the clearing, turning in a slow circle, and I wonder what its plan is.

As I take another arduous step toward the beast, my foot catches on a fallen branch. I am hurled forward, the ground rising to meet me.

I land face down, and the moment my injured leg connects with the ground, I hear a loud *snap* and then a primal roar. The sound comes from me. I am the one howling. Slowly, I curl in on myself and clutch my leg, too afraid to look at the damage my fall has caused. A steady whimper leaves my lips as I am unable to move.

There goes my chance to save the clan and prove my worth. They will surely send me back to that wretched bed where I can do nothing but watch life happen all around me.

I crane my head back, searching the training grounds for the draxilio. It must have heard my fall. I find an empty clearing.

But my mother, my father, and Varrek are at my side, all wearing matching looks of anger and concern.

They are shouting words at me, but I cannot hear them. The

constant throb of pain beats loudly in my ears and drowns out all sounds.

"What is the matter with you?" my father asks, turning me onto my back.

"My son. Why?" I hear my mother demand, her forehead creased with worry.

"You are the biggest fool I have ever known," Varrek scolds as he helps my father position me so my mother can examine my wound.

I am confused as to why Varrek is here. Shouldn't he be with Clohee? Did he not ask me to cover for him and oversee today's training?

I point a finger toward the clearing. "The… wait, the draxilio," I mumble, panting through the pain.

Varrek follows my finger, and looks back down at me, confused and irritated. "Draxilio? You saw one? Where?"

"It was… right there. On the training grounds. I swear it," I reply.

The three of them look back at the clearing, then at each other, but remain silent.

"I was merely trying to help you, brother," I mutter through gritted teeth.

"Help *me*? How is this helping me?" Varrek shouts.

My mother lightly presses the skin above and below my injury, looking it over, and her touch is excruciating. It takes all my willpower not to yell at the top of my lungs. "Yo-you asked me to take over today's training session, did you not?"

He jerks back, perplexed. "No. Absolutely not. Why would I ask you to lead a training session when your leg is still in such poor shape? What do you speak of, Ahlvo?"

"Son, you are barely able to hold yourself up in the washbox. You cannot even *participate* in a training session, much less lead it," my father adds.

I throw my head back onto the mossy ground as I try to recall Varrek's request. I search my memories… and find nothing. "I-I cannot remember."

"Oh, my son. You are disoriented. I was afraid this would happen," my mother says. "We gave you a slightly stronger dose of the sedative to help you sleep through the night. Clearly it did not work as intended."

I sigh in frustration. My mother's words make sense, which is unfortunate. This means that I was never healed enough to return to training. Varrek did not request my assistance in leading the crew. At no point was I well enough to even get out of bed and leave my mother's med room. Was the draxilio even there? Or was it merely an illusion brought on by a drug?

Anger fills my mind. It consumes my heart. It pumps through my blood. It's too much, too powerful. I do not know what to do with it, so I open my mouth wide and bellow into the trees above.

My mind has deceived me so spectacularly that my injury is now worse than before. Will I ever fully recover? Will I ever rejoin my crew out on the training grounds? Will I ever be a worthy male for my inara, my Aye-vah?

Just as images of her luminous brown eyes flood my mind, she appears at my side. Her tight curls jut out from her head every which way, fear and bewilderment scrunching her features. "What happened?" she cries.

"Let us take him back home," my mother says. "I cannot rebandage his leg here."

The four people who matter most to me huddle around my body and carry me. Outside the med room, my Aye-vah holds open the door for us to scoot past, worry covering her beautiful face.

I am gently lowered onto my bed as my mother and Aye-vah get to work removing my torn and dirt-covered bandage and replacing it with a clean one.

My father hands me a mug of water and orders me to drink. As I do, he puts a damp cloth on my forehead and pulls my braids away from my face. He must see panic in my eyes because he pats my arm comfortingly and says, "You will pull through, son. You will."

I see Varrek whispering something to Aye-vah as she grabs jars of healing salve from the shelf in the corner. Her facial expression morphs from shock, to disappointment, to sheer agony, and I assume he is recalling my ill-advised journey to the training grounds in the dark.

My mother leans over my exposed wound, examining it closely. "The surgical site is torn, and there appears to be some swelling."

"Do we need to put him into the med tube for further diagnostics or to repair the stitches?" Aye-vah asks as she rushes over with the salves.

"No. I do not think it is necessary," my mother says, all business. "We can clean and rebandage the wound and give him a dose of the fuutacalati to reduce inflammation."

I swallow hard and ask, "How much did this set me back?"

"I would guess half a moon cycle, maybe more. You were quite lucky," my mother says in a serious tone. "It could have been much worse." Yet the look she gives tells me she is afraid for me. There is also disappointment, and that crushes me more.

After my wound is cleaned and bandaged, my father takes a seat beside me as Varrek resumes his whispering to Aye-vah in the far corner of the room. Only now, my mother has joined them.

"What are they speaking of?" I ask aloud, not expecting my father to know the answer.

"I suppose it is about how stubborn and foolish you are, my son," he says flatly. "You know you cannot continue to fight your body. You will not win."

"I am a grown male. I have the ability to decide what is best for my body," I finally reply.

"Do you?"

Perhaps I do not but admitting it will surely feel like defeat. I can take no more of that, and so I say nothing.

The angry fog inside my mind rises anew. *You cannot decide what is best for your body. Look at yourself. Look at what you did tonight. You are a failure. You are worthless.*

Aye-vah, Varrek, and my mother abruptly cease their whispers and walk slowly toward me. My stomach twists itself in knots and sweat covers my palms.

"Ahlvo, in light of what happened, I—we," Varrek corrects, "we think it would be best for you to leave the village in order to complete your recovery."

I am stunned into silence. Many questions swirl inside my mind as the angry fog adds, *See? They do not want you here. You are a burden.*

"You want me to leave?" I mutter.

"Yes, we think being this close to the training grounds is particularly triggering for you. It's a constant reminder of what you can't do at the moment. Removing that trigger should allow you to focus on healing, and it will be better for your mental health," Aye-vah says in a serious tone she has never used on me. It is firm and devoid of emotion —clinical.

You are clearly a failure in her eyes as well, the fog continues. I grit my teeth.

"No, Varrek. This will leave the clan vulnerable," I point out. "The tr'gorys still surround us in the darkness. The draxil–"

"Ahlvo," Varrek interrupts, "we can handle those things while you recover."

He says he does not need you. That you cannot protect your clan. He is right, the fog notes.

"Where?" I choke out, unable to continue the fight to stay. "Where do you want me to go?"

"The dwelling by the lake. While you are there, you can update the comm system to reach us and Trovilia, replenish the sea stock, and complete some other minor repairs that Bruvix planned on doing during his annual visit," Varrek says, making it seem like this is an opportunity, rather than a punishment. "All of these tasks can be done while seated."

"I will ensure that you have all the medicines and supplies you need to care for your wound while you are away," my mother adds. She takes my hand and gives it a squeeze. "This will be good for you, my son."

My eyes dart between the three of them rapidly. I feel betrayed. I am sure they feel they are doing this for my benefit, but it does not feel that way to me. It feels as if I am being banished from my home, my clan, my family, and my inara, all because I am eager to return to my duties.

The fog takes their side. *You should stay there and never return. They do not want you here. They will be able to live happy lives once you are gone.*

Bile rises in my throat, and I feel ill. "Very well. Wh-when shall I leave?"

Varrek sighs. "Today."

CHAPTER 6

AVA

I hold the door open to the med room as the others carry in an injured Ahlvo from his trek toward the training grounds. Once they're safely inside the room, I dart around in a rush, my body shaking and adrenaline pumping in my hands and feet as I move. I'm careful to stay out of Kaiva's way as she removes Ahlvo's dirty bandages and examines his wound.

After throwing the torn and mud-covered bandages in the trash, I grab a stack of fresh ones from the shelf in the corner of the room. I'm on autopilot, and I'm grateful that I've dressed his wound enough times to know what to do without having to pause and wonder if the salve I reach for is the correct one.

Despite the fall, miraculously, Ahlvo didn't do too much damage to his wound. I shudder when I think of what could've happened if he'd landed wrong, or if he hit his head on a rock or… I can come up with so many terrible things. So many things that could've caused a major setback, or worse, in the short distance he traveled.

I try not to be mad at Varrek, but I am. At least part of me is. *How* could he have slept through all the racket Ahlvo must've made when he was trying to leave? He was supposed to be keeping an eye on Ahlvo so I could be with Kate and finally get some quality shut-eye.

And yet, here I am, rebandaging Ahlvo's open and angry-looking wound all because Varrek is a heavy sleeper.

Ugh, I know it's not his fault, but my mind is reeling, and I feel helpless and frustrated.

"He cannot go on like this," Varrek whispers.

"I know," I sigh. "But I don't know what more we can do to help him. He's just… fixated on being able to train again."

"He said he saw a draxilio," Varrek scoffs.

"Wait, what?" I ask, goose bumps covering my arms.

"No, it was an illusion. There was nothing there," Varrek replies. "Do you think my presence possibly contributed to this story he created?"

I ponder this. "It's possible. I think it's hard for him to see everybody going about their lives while he's stuck in that bed. It's like he doesn't know who he is if he can't help you protect the clan."

Varrek rubs a hand down his face. "Well, there is nothing that can be done about that as long as he is bedridden."

I rush over to Kaiva with fresh bandages and salve. She takes them from me without letting her gaze stray from the wound. Her work is quick and silent, and I hand her the supplies she needs during each step of the process.

When Ahlvo's wound is rebandaged, Kaiva and I wash up, then we tidy the countertop as Rumo sits with Ahlvo on the other side of the room. Varrek sidles up to us, his face still scrunched in worry, and whispers, "What if we sent him to the dwelling by the lake? He would be away from here, away from the constant reminders of what he cannot do."

"I worry how that kind of isolation would affect him. It could very easily send him in the wrong direction," I add.

My eyes glance at our difficult patient as he settles on the bed; he knows we're discussing him. Kaiva wipes the sweat off her brow and releases a breath. "Even somewhere else, I do not trust my son to honor and respect his current limitations. He is a stubborn male. And I know where he gets it from…" she trails off. Her eyes narrow at Rumo at first, but then the corner of her mouth curls up in a grin.

I can't help but watch her loving gaze as it holds her mate. They are ridiculously cute together even after I-don't-know-how-many years.

Then it hits me.

"I'll go with him," I whisper to Varrek and Kaiva. "I'll keep an eye on him, and I won't let him sabotage his recovery."

Varrek scoffs, skepticism swirling in his eyes. "He will not want you to be taken away from the clan to be his personal healer. That will make him feel ashamed, even more than he already does."

"There's no other option," I mutter. "He can't go out there alone, and he can't stay here."

"How do you plan on convincing him to let you go along?" Kaiva asks.

I run through all the ways to best approach the subject with Ahlvo. "I don't."

Kaiva and Varrek give me matching looks of utter confusion. Even though Ahlvo watches us closely, unhappy to be left out of the conversation, I gesture for them to lean their heads closer to mine and whisper, "I have a plan."

CHAPTER 7

AHLVO

The bed I have been desperate to get out of for weeks makes a creaking sound as I shift to a seated position. Since my fall in the early hours of the morning, everyone has been busy preparing for my departure.

I made a second attempt to convince Varrek that I must stay here, but that conversation ended the moment he brought up the draxilio hallucination. No response seemed adequate, so I gave none.

I have been told explicitly not to move from my bed, so this is where I have remained, still and quiet. Unease fills my belly with each passing minute. I rub the edge of my thin blanket between my fingers, wishing I could remain here with my family, my clan, and most importantly, with Aye-vah. But Varrek has determined it would be best for me, and the clan, if I complete my recovery at the dwelling by the lake. Away from here.

If I had a valid argument to counter Varrek's decision, I would offer it, but he is right. I have been miserable since the moment I awoke and looked down at the mess that was once my strong leg. I have been a difficult patient. A very difficult patient, actually. My mother and Aye-vah have spent each day caring for me, trying to make me feel better about my circumstances, and I have been nothing but a surly encumbrance.

You deserve to be banished, the angry fog sneers. *No one wants you around.*

I run my fingers through my mane and sigh, too tired to try to silence the angry fog with rational, positive thoughts. Perhaps it is right, and I should not fight it anymore.

My mother comes down the stairs with two sacks in her hands. "This one—" she lifts the bag in her right hand "—has fresh clothes. And this one—" she lifts the left, "—has fresh wraps, salves, and medicines to keep your wound clean and your pain minimal until you return home."

She drops the sacks next to the bed and tilts her head, thoughtfully. "Do you need instructions on how to administer the medicines? I can create a recording on one of these screen pads, if you would like?"

"No, that will not be necessary. I have seen how you and Aye-vah do it and will remember how to do it myself," I assure her in a quiet voice.

She rubs my shoulder and gives me a warm, motherly glance. "This time away will be good for your spirit, my son. And your body."

"Yes, and for everyone else's spirits, as well," I mutter. Bitterness and disappointment run through my veins, and I am certain both were present in my tone just now. But it does not matter. Soon I shall be gone, and my clan can rest easy.

The fog adds, *Yes, they will be glad you are no longer here constantly ruining things.*

My mother's face falls, and just as she is about to offer comforting words, Nalba bursts through the door.

"Ahlvo! Come, come. I have made something for you," she exclaims, pulling my mother out the front door. I hobble behind on my crutch.

Nalba's creations are often spectacular, even if they are visually underwhelming. She is famous for her hidden compartments, trick functions, and simple-yet-sophisticated design. But the moment I hop outside and my eyes land on the item she made for me, I am… confused.

"What is this?" I ask with a tight smile. I am trying to understand what I am looking at, but unlike her other inventions with clear, mundane purposes, I see only slabs of steel welded together to make an interesting shape.

"It is a hover seat! Much like an air bicycle without wheels." She points at the steel contraption with glee, and then rolls her eyes at my lack of enthusiasm. "O fah. Allow me to demonstrate."

She throws her leg over the center of the horizontal steel bench and presses a button on the tall handle that rises in front of her chest. With a loud clang, a long slab folds out on the right side of the bench, and Nalba says, "This is for your injured leg. Rest it here." There is a small pedal at the bottom of the handle, and Nalba places her left foot on it, showing me where to place my good leg. Then she presses the big green button in the center of the handle, and the entire thing lifts off the ground. It does not lift to the standard height of an air bicycle. This one hovers up to my knee.

Nalba's face contorts into the biggest smile I have ever seen as she slowly turns and moves the hover seat back and forth in the air. "Eh?"

After a few moments of this, she lands it, and the device hits the ground with a thud. "I did not have enough time to make it lift higher, so only use it for short distances and above relatively small obstacles. The engine cannot handle much more than that."

Varrek and my father stride toward us with matching expressions of excitement as they watch Nalba get off the hover seat. "Ah! So it is complete, Nalba?" Varrek asks, clasping his hands together.

"Yes, I was showing Ahlvo how to use it."

My father gives the hover seat a closer inspection, shaking it and checking Nalba's welding work. "Exceptional, Nalba," he says.

Then he turns to me. "We removed the front seat in the zip ship so you can fit this behind the command levers. You are able to glide it directly into the ship and remain seated for the journey."

They have thought of everything. I suppose, under any other

circumstance, I would be grateful for their help and thoughtfulness to ensure my comfort while I am away.

The sooner they get you out of here, the sooner they can return to their lives. You are holding them back, the angry fog mutters in a sour tone.

"Right. Well, I suppose it is time to depart," I say.

Cloh-ee and Kay-teh emerge onto the main path, and Bruvix arrives from the other direction moments later. I am surrounded by members of my clan that I am closest to, with one very notable exception.

I scan the village and the surrounding woods for her dark, fluffy curls. Nothing. "Where is Aye-vah?"

Cloh-ee and my mother exchange panicked looks, and when they turn to face me, their eyes swirl with what appears to be sympathy. "She is at the waterfall, collecting nilakovaye seeds for more healing salve. We are nearly out," my mother stammers.

Cloh-ee adds with an encouraging smile, "Yeah, she wishes she could be here, but she told me to tell you to be careful and get well soon."

My heart sinks.

Being away from my inara with be difficult enough—with the mating bond incomplete, our tether strengthens with each passing day. The intensity of it has been dulled by the medicines in my blood, but it will continue to strengthen the longer we wait. She may not feel our mate bond—I do not think Cloh-ee could feel it with Varrek—but I do. And being away from Aye-vah for an unknown period of time will crush me.

She did not even want to say good-bye…

The angry fog scoffs, *Because she is tired of your whining.*

"Very well," I say coldly. I try to conceal my disappointment by shaking out my shoulders and getting onto the hover seat.

"Uh… I think I'll say good-bye right here, if that's okay," Kay-teh says in a shaky voice. She knows we are about to leave the safety of our village, and with her draxilio sightings, she is afraid.

"I'll stay here with her," Cloh-ee adds, putting a supportive arm around Kay-teh's small rounded shoulders.

They run up to me and wrap their tiny arms around me tightly. "Feel better, Ahlvo," and "Miss you already," are whispered in my ears before they back away.

"Thank you both. I shall return soon." I give them a warm smile, as warm as I can anyway, before continuing on the main path of the village toward the clearing where our ships are kept outside the forest.

I pass members of the clan on my hover seat as they stand on the edge of the path. They wave, their faces tight with sympathy, and I want to tell them to look away, to spare me their pity. Instead, I growl under my breath and wave back.

I hear Varrek tell his mate that he will be back as soon as possible, and my muscles clench with envy at the bond he has with Cloh-ee. I should have that with Aye-vah. But I do not, because she has no idea what she is to me.

She does not want you anyway, the fog adds.

Once we arrive at the zip ship, my father, Varrek, and Bruvix load my belongings into the back storage compartment of the small vessel as Nalba and my mother help me settle my hover seat behind the controls.

Bruvix reaches into the ship where I am seated and grips my shoulder. "I shall make a special batch of ale for your return, to celebrate your healed leg."

"I hope it does not taste like slug piss this time," I tease.

Bruvix's scarred face twists up in annoyance, and he steps back next to my mother.

Varrek takes his place, and for a moment, we are silent. "We shall pray to the goddess for your swift recovery, brother," he says finally.

"I thank you for that," I tell him.

He clears his throat and his gaze darts away from mine. "While you are away, I have decided to make Bruvix my second-in-command. This is temporary, and it is merely to ensure the safety of the clan."

I expected as much, though my hands still tighten into fists at the news. It is right for the clan. "I understand," I tell him.

You were just relieved of your duties to protect the clan. You are officially useless, the fog says. *Do not bother returning to the village. Bruvix will do a better job than you ever could.*

Varrek gives me a single nod, and is about to step back, but I stop him. "Please, take care of Aye-vah while I am away."

He blinks at me and then says, "I shall. Certainly."

I wave good-bye to each of them, and once they are a safe distance from the ship, I start the engine and launch into the sky above the tree line.

Part of me, a very large part, is tempted to look back at those I hold closest to my heart to see if Aye-vah has joined them at the last moment, but I do not because I know she is not there. She did not wish to see me off, and I do not need the painful reminder as my journey begins.

* * *

Hours later, I arrive at the lake dwelling and land the zip ship on the large flattened patch of grass and sand just outside the front door. I shut down the ship, still reeling from negative thoughts that filled my mind during my journey. The angry fog was eager to fill the silence of the ship with cruel words, and I let it.

I was also surrounded by Aye-vah's sweet scent the entire way, which was as confusing as it was irritating. I do not know if it was my imagination—another drug-induced hallucination, perhaps—or because her scent is deeply embedded in my belongings due to the time she spends in my mother's med room. Either way, it was hard to focus on anything other than how much I already miss her. How the fog knows I'm not worthy.

Now I am in a particularly sour mood and want nothing more than to collapse onto the bed and sleep these thoughts away.

After bumping the interior sides of the ship a few times, I maneuver my hover seat outside and guide it toward the front door of the dwelling. Once inside, I toss in two douku orbs to add light and check for signs of possible intruders, past and present. Upon finding none, I lean off the edge of my hover seat and get to work, starting a fire in the pit.

This home is a single room with only one level. A small square table sits between the spigot and the fire pit, making up the meal area. There is a large wash basin and waste box behind a folding door off to the side. Against the back wall in the corner is the bed piled high with cushions and furs. It is a welcome sight to my eyes.

I guide my hover seat over to the side of the bed and park it there. Then I reach up and tug my braids free, one by one. Normally, I prefer to keep my braids neat and tidy—manes have always been a way to showcase drive and character on Trovilia, and as a male who grew up without wealth or status, it was the only way to prove my worth to onlookers—but here, in this lonely space, I have no one to impress, and no mirrors to remind me of the mess I have become. Here, my mane can become as tangled as the feelings whirling within me.

With a shake, my mane falls in waves around my shoulders, and I hurl myself off the hover seat and onto the bed with a grunt. I sigh as I tug my tunic and pants off, toe off my boots, and pull a fur over my stomach. I'm ready to sleep, to do nothing...

There is a clink. It sounds the moment my boot hits the floor next to my hover seat, and when I lean over the edge to investigate, I find a container filled with liquid.

It is a jar of ale, still sealed. Bruvix must have left this here on his last trip.

I smile at the perfect timing of this unexpected gift and pull the top off, pouring its contents down my throat in three gulps. My throat burns as the ale makes its way toward my stomach.

Aye-vah would not be pleased to witness this.

But she is not here, the fog points out. *She is back in the village, thrilled that you are gone.*

I feel relieved and surprisingly happy as I stare at the empty jar. Happy to have finally arrived, and happy that exhaustion is pulling me away from this day and into the next.

CHAPTER 8

AVA

Well, this was a terrible idea. Where the fuck is he?

Another shiver rips through my body, and as my teeth clatter, I curse inwardly at my very stupid plan to stay hidden in the back of the ship and pop out like a stripper from a cake when Ahlvo comes to unload his luggage. It's been at least an hour since we arrived at the lake house, and Ahlvo hasn't been back to get the bags. I know there's food in here because I've already stress-eaten some junasii bread and other snacks he should've taken inside immediately, but... nope. Clearly he just went inside and parked himself somewhere and has no intention of coming back out anytime soon.

The storage compartment of this tiny ship is separated from the seating area by a grayish partition that I can only sort of see through. I can't get a clear view beyond the ship, even with the massive wind-shield, but I can see shadows. And with the darkness and cold air that's been steadily creeping in over the last twenty minutes, I know it's nighttime.

A wave of homesickness washes over me when I think of my warm bed back in the village and my good-byes to Kate and Chloe. Before I climbed into the back of the zip ship, they hugged me so tight, I couldn't breathe.

Okay, time for a game plan, I remind myself.

I'm surrounded by boxes and large bags of supplies, and it's cramped as hell back here. I'm confident that I could dig out some blankets and safely stay in here overnight, but I really, *really,* don't want to do that. Especially since I've been back here for several hours and my feet are asleep. Maybe in my early twenties I could've managed it, but at thirty-two, my back will be stiff for days if I even briefly sit the wrong way in a chair. I need to move around. I need to pee. And I really need to check on Ahlvo.

Shifting smaller boxes from one side of the ship's trunk to the other, I clear myself a narrow path to the back hatch. I can't see very well, but the ship's console gives off enough reddish light that I can see directly in front of me.

Slow and steady, girl, I tell myself.

The second I move, heavy rain patters against the ship's exterior.

I roll my eyes. *You've gotta be fucking kidding me.*

Briefly, I ponder staying in here and waiting out the rain. But now that we're officially in Oluura's wet season, it could be hours before the rain lets up. Or maybe even days. I need to make my move now.

I squeeze my plump arms and wide hips through the narrow clearing I made to the hatch and tug on the metal handle. Nothing.

Rising to a crouch, I pull again, this time using both hands. There's a slight give to it, but not enough to open. I try again with more of an upward heave, but the handle still doesn't budge.

The rain has picked up, now dumping buckets from the sky, and clearly my puny human muscles are not enough to open this hatch, so I nudge the boxes and bags aside, making space, and drop to my hands and knees. I wiggle my way down until I'm lying on my left side. Lifting my right leg, I line it up so I can press the ball of my foot against the underside of the handle. Bracing against the floor, I pull my leg back and kick the handle with as much force as I can muster.

The handle moves, finally, but not quite enough. I kick again, and again, until I hear the click of the internal latch releasing and the hatch lifts open.

It's still pouring, but luckily, the cover of the hatch keeps me dry while I sit up and scoot out of the ship. Something thin and curved catches on my ankle when I swing my legs out in front of me. It falls from the compartment, landing in the mud with a *splat*.

I sigh. None of this is going according to plan. But I lightly place my booted feet on either side of the mud puddle, and I blindly reach my hand into the mud and feel around.

"Blech, ohmygodohmygodohmygod," I mumble in disgust. After a minute or so of wiggling my fingers in a deep puddle of what feels like chunky pudding, I find it. It's a cord of some kind, and when I look at my prize, I find it's completely caked in mud and wrapped in blades of grass.

"Hope this isn't important," I say to no one. Then I place the dirty cord on the floor of the ship and carefully hop out into the rainstorm. I brush my muddy hand on my pants, take a deep breath, and shut the hatch of the ship before sprinting toward the door.

Fewer than ten steps from the door, I slip. With hands flailing, I land on my ass in the mud, splashing dirty water all over my face and hair.

I get up slowly, checking for any injuries, thankfully finding none. The rain intensifies, doing more to spread the mud than rinse it. Letting a stream of curses fly, I storm toward the door and fling it open.

I'm cold, drenched, covered in muck, and that is only after I've been locked in a cold, empty ship for over an hour. A steady groan emanates from my throat as I adjust to the dim light of the douku orbs sitting on the floor near the water spigot. Frustration expands like a balloon inside my chest as my eyes search the rest of the cabin for Ahlvo, and then I find him, peacefully passed out on the bed.

He appears to have an empty glass jar in his hand and a fur blanket that does nothing to cover his very naked body. What was in that jar? Alcohol? Was he drinking?

I sniff the air, and sure enough, I detect the bitter scent of Bruvix's ale. Unfucking-believable. Apparently, the moment he's unsupervised, he leans into the darkness inside his mind and seeks recklessness.

Don't we all? I say to myself, which is, of course, true, but Ahlvo had no idea I was tagging along on this trip. How deep would he have let himself sink? The thought terrifies me.

I slam the door shut behind me and yell "Hey!" at the top of my lungs. Mid-snore, Ahlvo snaps up, his mouth still agape and his eyes narrowed in confusion.

"Bikar? Aye-vah?" He rubs his eyes and leans up to a seated position. "Why are you covered in gloop?"

"Oh, hey there, Ahlvo. Did I wake you? *So* sorry," I sneer. "Wouldn't want to interrupt your relaxing getaway or anything. I was just locked in the back of your ship all day, hoping to surprise you when you came to take in the supplies, which includes your sleep medication, by the way, but it seems you'd rather soothe your aches and pains with alcohol than use the stuff your body needs."

My tone is dripping with disdain, but at this point, I don't care. "Don't mind me though. I'll just be over here trying to find my skin under the three-hundred layers of mud I've got on me."

He stares at me blankly, and then asks, "Are you a dream?"

Seriously? Even when I want to verbally rip him to shreds, he has to say something cute.

"No, not a dream, Ahlvo," I say stiffly, grabbing a towel from a hook by the door and wiping off my hands. "I came with you. I hid in the back of the ship. I'm here to be with you while you heal."

He smiles, and his eyes go dreamy. He scoots to the edge of the bed, and mindful of his leg, reaches for his crutch. He stands and the blanket that was barely covering his muscled thigh falls away. "You came here… for me?" he asks, placing a hand over his heart.

Argh. I want to stay mad. I still smell booze and want to continue yelling. But he's grinning from ear to ear, and my eyes are desperate to zero in on that hog hanging between his legs.

Okay focus, Ava.

I put a hand up, blocking the magnificent view and say, "First things first: you need to cover your junk."

CHAPTER 9

AHLVO

I stand there, my mind still abuzz from the ale, and continue to blink at Aye-vah. She is here. Truly here in the dwelling by the lake. My inara is standing before me, but my mind does not wish to believe my eyes. Yet, Aye-vah has insisted that this is not a dream, so I continue staring at her, not knowing what to say.

Her hair hangs in damp tendrils around her face, and from the neck down, she is covered in dirt. Initially, I am angry at that dirt for blocking my view of this luminous female, but then I realize she must have fallen. She could be injured.

"Are you hurt? Did something happen?" I ask, gesturing to her mud-soaked clothing. I take another step closer, the drive to care for her pushing me forward.

"Junk, Ahlvo! Cover it. Please," Aye-vah shouts with a hand up. I am confused by her phrasing, though.

"This word means trash?" I look around, seeking the rubbish that has offended my mate, but I find nothing.

"No, no, no. Among humans, it also means private parts."

"I–I, um…" I trail off, still confused.

"Your penis! Please cover yourself," Aye-vah clarifies with a snicker.

"Oh." Now I understand. My pants are on the floor next to the bed. I do not have the balance to bend over and retrieve them without falling, so I grab the fur and wrap it around my lower half. I hold it against my hip and hobble my way over to Aye-vah.

She is still blocking her view of me with her hand, so when I take that hand in mine and lower it, a shocked gasp slips out of her. "I did not mean to frighten you." I reach up and stroke a smear of mud from her cheek with my thumb. "Are you all right?"

Her big brown eyes hold mine for a moment before she blinks rapidly and jerks away from my touch. "No, Ahlvo, I'm not all right."

I go to ask her what is wrong, but she cuts me off.

"I'm soaking wet, dirty, exhausted, and sore from crouching in the back of the zip ship for hours. I'm also freezing, hungry, and have to pee," she says as she paces angrily across the kitchen area. "Also? I'm extremely disappointed to find that the second you got here, you started drinking, which is precisely what we've asked you *not* to do. Why are you so determined to sabotage yourself?"

She is worried for me. She wants me to succeed and recover, and here I am deliberately ignoring her instructions to soothe my own pain. What she does not realize is that my pain is the direct result of the belief she did not wish to say good-bye to me. "Well, I did not think—"

"You know what? It doesn't even matter," she interrupts, waving her hands dismissively. "I'm here now. And guess what? I care enough about your recovery for both of us, and I am *not* going to let you fail."

I try to keep my face neutral, despite the flips and twists of my stomach. Aye-vah cares about me. She cares about me a lot. I knew this, of course, because of the time we have spent together. But the fury I now see in her eyes at the thought of me hurting myself, it feels new. More.

Could she… Does she sense the tether between us?

She huffs out a breath and kicks off her muddy boots before making her way to the wash basin. We are both silent as she turns the handle of the spigot, holding a finger beneath the stream of water for a few moments until she deems the temperature acceptable.

I point to a stack of towels near the bed, and she hastily grabs two. "I'm going to take a bath. We'll discuss this later," she grumbles before pulling the folding door closed behind her.

Aye-vah is mad at me, yet I am filled with joy. I grin widely, relieved that I no longer need to hide it, and place my tunic on the hook outside the door for her. In the morning, I shall grab my extra clothing along with the other supplies still inside the ship. To think she'd been in there all that time…

I make my way back to the bed, placing the empty mug on the hover seat, and once seated, I tug my pants on and slip under the furs. I have learned that human females are not comfortable with male nudity, so I shall remain covered until I win her heart. Now that she is here, and it is just the two of us, I might have a chance.

No, you do not. She does not want you, the angry fog whispers. But I do my best to push the thoughts away, because my inara came here to care for me, and to the best of my ability, I shall do the same for her.

Aye-vah exits the washroom several minutes later surrounded by a cloud of steam. Her glowing brown skin is dappled with drops of water, and her hair is clean and hanging in tight wet curls around her face. She steals my breath, this female.

She keeps a clenched fist on the edge of the towel wrapped around her chest as she scans the cabin nervously.

"I left my tunic on the hook for you," I tell her, knowing that was the source of her unease.

"Oh," she says quietly as she grabs it, "thank you."

She rushes back into the washroom to change and when she returns, she looks far more comfortable wearing my tunic. It's loose everywhere and hits just above her knees.

The sight of her in my clothes, covered in my scent, does something to me. Something primal. It makes me want to sink my fangs into her shoulder, marking her as mine forever.

"Only one bed?" Aye-vah asks, shaking me from my thoughts.

"Yes, but I am prepared to be a generous bed mate," I reply with a cheeky smirk.

She rolls her eyes but makes her way to the other side of the bed.

She climbs under the furs, remaining on the far edge of her side, seemingly determined to avoid any physical contact with me whatsoever.

That is fine. I can wait.

I reach into the pocket of my pants and pull out a small vial. "I did not leave all of my medicine on the ship. Should I still take this?"

"How much of that ale did you have?"

"Only a jar's worth," I tell her, pointing to the jar.

"Well," she says with an exasperated sigh, "it should be okay, but to be safe, only take half."

I do as she says, and I place the half-empty vial next to the empty jar.

Aye-vah gives me a half smile, but she turns over, facing away from me.

"Aye-vah?" I ask.

"Yes?"

"I am glad you are here."

Aye-vah makes a soft sound, a grunt that still somehow sounds angelic, and says, "Me too, bud. Me too."

CHAPTER 10

AVA

Five more minutes. Just five more minutes, and then I'll get this day started, I vow to myself as I snuggle deeper into my pillow. But when the pillow snuggles back and pulls me closer, my eyes open in alarm.

I look up, and Ahlvo gives me a sleepy smile. "Morivikka, Aye-vah."

Backing away, pulling out of his arms, I move as far over on my side of the bed as I can without falling off. "Huh. So that happened."

"What?"

"Um, the cuddling. We can't be doing that!" I shriek, my voice rough from lack of hydration.

Ahlvo props himself up on his elbows and tilts his head at me, curiously. "I did not do that, Aye-vah. *You* noodled your way over to *my* side of the bed and put your head on my chest."

I don't remember doing that, but I went to bed freezing and Ahlvo's body is like a bulky, delicious radiator, so I'm not entirely surprised that's how we ended up.

He's smirking at me now, all male smugness. Part of me wants to call him a liar, another part of me wants to smack him, and a very small part (okay, a big part) of me wants to climb back over to his side and tuck my body against his because it felt like a dream.

Admittedly, I have fantasized about what it would be like to snuggle with him. How can I not when I've spent so many nights in the med room beside him? Actually, I expected it to be somewhat uncomfortable because he's so cut and heavily muscled. I figured it would be like using a brick as a pillow with several more bricks as a mattress. But it wasn't like that at all.

His skin is soft, like velvet and leather, and covering his hard pectorals and abs is a layer of fat that makes him extra cuddly. The cushiness might be due to his lack of exercise training with the crew, but whatever it is, it makes me want to spend the rest of my days pressed against him.

That can't happen, I tell myself. *You're not his inara. She's still out there, and if or when he finds her, it will crush you if you get too attached.*

Right.

I push away the memory of his warmth and place three pillows in the center of the bed. "There," I say resolutely. "Now, we have a divider."

"Whatever you wish." Ahlvo chuckles, and maybe it's just because I can still feel the heat of his skin against mine, but the deep and throaty sound makes my pussy flutter.

I pause for a moment to listen for rain. Upon hearing none, I clap my hands together, grateful for the distraction of a to-do list. "Shall we unload the ship before it starts raining again?" I ask.

"Yes, we shall," he replies, rubbing a hand down his abs, and I fight the urge to clench my thighs. "Then we must eat. I am ravenous."

My stomach growls in response, and while I'm embarrassed, at least it's a bodily instinct I can indulge.

If Ahlvo heard it, he doesn't call attention to it. He pulls himself onto his hover seat with minimal effort and turns the machine around, facing me. "Let us complete this task so we may feast."

I tug my boots on, and as we make our way outside, I marvel at how smoothly Ahlvo navigates the hover seat. Nalba really is a genius. The fact that the entire thing lifts into mid-air, but just high enough to avoid stairs or uneven terrain, makes it an incredibly innovative mode of transportation. He can go almost anywhere on it. Plus, it has a storage compartment on the back and a hook on the side to attach his crutch.

Is this why he seems to be in such a good mood? Because he's finally able to move around?

"So how do you like the hover seat?" I ask as he lifts the back hatch of the ship easily.

He surveys the supplies and says, "It is quite efficient." He pulls the heaviest sacks onto his lap, piling them on his thighs and I wince on his behalf. Doesn't that hurt?

"I can take those, Ahlvo. I don't want you to overdo it."

He stares at me blankly, and then tugs one of the bags off his lap and hands it to me. "Okay, then," he says.

I take the handle and the moment he lets go, gravity takes over and the bag lands hard on the still-damp ground. "Jesus, what the fuck is in here? Boulders?"

Ahlvo laughs. "Tools," he says.

He pulls the bag from the ground and brushes the dirt from the bottom of it. "I may not be able to use my leg, Aye-vah, but that does not mean the strength has left my body." He returns the heavy bag to his lap and takes a medium-sized box in one hand. "I am capable of carrying a great amount of weight in my arms without much effort." He lifts the box over his head, and then back down to his side like it's a five-pound dumbbell. His bicep flexes, growing to the size of both my thunder thighs pressed together. Then he turns and glides the hover seat toward the house.

I suppress the urge to groan as my toes curl inside my boots. What is he doing to me? You can't say stuff like that to a fat girl and then show her how much weight you can lift with just one hand. Doesn't he realize I'm going to be turned on for the rest of the day now?

I distract myself by moving the boxes around, pulling the smaller ones forward and pushing the heavier boxes off to the side. There's no real reason for this other than desperately needing something to do with my hands. I reach for my bag of clothes and another bag that I think holds Ahlvo's bandages and salves and follow behind his hover seat as he heads back inside.

We work together like this for another hour or so, him carrying the heavy stuff and me grabbing the lighter bags until the ship is empty and our stuff is in piles just inside the front door.

He carefully arranges a series of tools on a ledge between the only window in the cabin and a wooden box sticking out of the wall, and then turns to me with a very dirty cord in his hand. "What happened to this?"

"I, uh, I dropped it in the mud. It's not important, is it?"

"Well, it is the cable that opens the comm line from here to the village and also to Trovilia," he says, not an ounce of frustration in his tone.

But I still feel bad about ruining it. It was the main task he was supposed to accomplish while he's here. "Sorry about that."

Ahlvo examines the cord closely, brushing dirt off and picking at the ends of the cord. "No bother. I am sure there is something we can do."

I release a mock gasp. "Is that optimism I hear? Wow, Ahlvo. Just one day by the lake and you're already back to your old self."

He smiles, but it falls as his gaze turns stormy. "I would not say that."

I watch him, trying to think of something clever to say to bring back his smile. Then I notice his hair. His braids have been taken out, and it falls in black, slightly frizzy waves down his back and over his shoulders. It's wild and messy. I love it.

"Took your braids out, huh?"

He lifts a hand to his hair, fluffing a few strands, and for a split second, I could swear that he looks ashamed. "Yes, I… I don't—"

"It's cool," I interrupt. "You look like a lion."

"Lye-ohn?" he repeats slowly. "This is an animal from your planet?"

"Yep," I say. "One of the most fierce. Also known as 'king of beasts.'"

A grin slowly spreads across Ahlvo's face as he looks down at his injured leg. "I like that. Very much."

My gaze lingers on his messy hair as memories of the night we met flood my mind.

* * *

ONE MONTH AGO...

"Let go of that banana! It's for the octopus!" Kate bellows in her sleep as her body quivers. I've tried waking her, rubbing her back, and even responding to her bizarre sleep chatter, but I've found that the best thing to do is leave her be. The dream will end, and she'll slip back into a deep sleep.

It also means I haven't had a quality REM cycle since I was kidnapped from Earth and auctioned off to a pair of beefy gold aliens who swear Kate, Chloe, and I are not destined to become their sex slaves. They seem genuine, but I have my doubts. I have many doubts, actually.

"You stole my plunger, you skank," Kate mumbles as I pad over to the door of our small room on the ship. I hope she remembers the details of this dream because I have questions.

Once the door slides open, I step into the hallway and head toward the food hall. Since I can't sleep, I might as well snack, especially after spending the last week trapped in a glass cage with stale kibble as my only source of sustenance. I can still feel the chalky crumbles sticking to the roof of my mouth. Not even a heaping bowl of mac and cheese could erase that taste from my memory, I'm sure of it.

I can't remember where Ahlvo and Varrek keep the plates, so I take a piece of that sweet bread they fed us earlier and place it on a cloth napkin. After quietly opening a few cupboards, I find the cups and pour myself some tea. But as I fantasize about more of my favorite comfort foods, ones that I'll probably never taste again, I miss the cup and pour the piping hot tea onto my thumb.

"Shitshitshit!" I whisper-scream as the cup slips from my grasp

and clatters to the floor, spilling the tea everywhere. Discovering the cup didn't break, I breathe a sigh of relief even while cursing inwardly at the mess. Thank god no one else was here to see it.

"Causing chaos already, little human?"

I whip around to see a bare-chested Ahlvo leaning against the doorframe, giving me a big teasing grin. I half expect the doorframe to crack under the weight of his massive body. He's a big dude—extra large everywhere, if the thick outline stretching down his thigh is what I think it is.

"You cannot sleep, Aye-vah?" he asks softly as he enters. He's barefoot and wearing a pair of loose pants that hang just below his sculpted and delicious eight-pack. He strides over with the grace of a puma and leans down with a cloth napkin to help me wipe up my mess.

"Nah. Kate's a bit of a sleep talker, so I thought I'd grab a bite until she quiets down," I tell him as I try not to notice how close his hand is to mine. I try not to think about how much bigger it is in comparison, and I really try not to think about how it would feel to have those hands on me.

Maybe it's Stockholm syndrome, or maybe it's just a good ol' fashioned crush, but I can't seem to keep my eyes off this one. And I don't understand it at all. Actually I do, because he's gorgeous, but this is not the right time to catch feelings. I shouldn't feel anything but wary in Ahlvo's presence, but the wariness seems to be taking a backseat to attraction. His whole vibe puts me at ease, and that's an entirely new feeling for me—a welcome feeling.

"Sorry if I woke you up," I mutter to Ahlvo as we finish wiping up the tea.

"It is no bother, Aye-vah," Ahlvo promises. "I do not sleep well when I am away from home. Once I heard you stirring, I wanted to make sure you were all right."

That's kind of sweet.

"Aside from you know, everything, I'm doing fine. Thanks," I say dryly.

He holds my gaze for a moment, clearly not knowing what to say. "Space can be treacherous for beautiful beings like us."

He says it with such sincerity that it completely catches me off guard. Then a loud giggle escapes my lips. "You're too kind... and modest," I tease.

I realize we're still wiping up the spill, even though the floor is now clean and dry. He must see it too.

Ahlvo rises to stand, and I follow. As he straightens to his full height, the handle on the cabinet door I left ajar snags one of his braids and he lets out a frustrated grunt. He yanks his head forward to release it, and the door swings completely open, bopping him on the back of the head.

"Oh no! Don't move. I got it," I say, reaching up to free his hair.

Upon examination, his hair is seriously tangled around the handle. How the heck did he even do this? "Okay, give me a minute here."

"I can do it," he mutters, reaching up to pull on his braid.

I swat his hands away. "Uh, uh, uh! I've got it. Let me noodle around a bit."

"Noo-duhl? This is a food, yes? You wish to put food in my mane?" he asks, looking puzzled.

"No, I just need to noodle with it. You know?" I say, trying to show him in a hand gesture that "noodle around" means to fuss over something.

His lips stretch wide in a smile as he mimics my wiggle. "Just noodle with it?" he asks, followed by a low chuckle. "Very well, sweet Aye-vah. Noodle away."

Eventually, I free his hair from the handle, and Ahlvo studies the frayed and wavy end with a frown.

"Want me to fix it? I'm a good braider. I've been doing my own hair since I was a kid," I tell him.

He reaches out and strokes a lock of my hair while his intense violet eyes hold mine. "Your mane is thick like mine. It is lovely."

I stare at him, lips slightly parted at his unexpected compliment. Normally, when a stranger touches my hair, I go into a full-body clench while holding back a scream. But Ahlvo doesn't feel like a stranger, and his gaze is full of adoration, not unsettling fascination.

"Come with me, little noodle," Ahlvo says as he fills two cups with

tea and leads me, with my bread in hand, out of the food hall. We reach the bridge, and he puts our cups on the floor behind the command chairs. He pulls a blanket from a drawer hidden along the wall and spreads it out.

"Join me?" he asks with that charming grin of his as he plops down on the blanket as if this were a picnic. In space.

I hesitate. This is starting to feel like a date, and I'm no way prepared to date an alien. However, the windshield, or whatever it's called on a spaceship, is massive, and our view of the stars is breathtaking. But I can go with the flow, and if I need to establish boundaries with Ahlvo, I will. I can always throw the hot tea in his face if he gets frisky.

He gives me a knowing glance and drops his hands in his lap. "I see trepidation in your eyes, and I understand it. You do not trust me. I have not earned it. But I would never cause you harm, and I will say this until it eases your nerves, until my actions speak for me."

He's right, I don't trust him, but his words do put me at ease. I pray to whatever god exists out here that he's telling the truth.

"Here, let me fix your braid first," I say, dropping to my knees on the blanket right behind him. He's so damn tall; I have to reach up to play with his hair. I stroke my fingers through the ends of the braid and pull the wavy strands free. Once I get to the part of the braid that's still tight and clean, I weave the sections back together, my fingers flying, the familiar task settling my anxious thoughts.

"I thank you for fixing my mane. I am not sure I can explain it properly but keeping my braids neat is quite important to me," he says softly.

"No need to explain. I get it," I tell him. He has no idea just how much I get it, but I do. I've been judged by the neatness of my hair, or perceived lack thereof, more times than I can count.

I finish his braid and ask for a hair tie, and Ahlvo hands me a strand of wiry string. Rather than tying the string in a knot to hold it in place, the wiriness makes it easy to just wrap around the end of the braid like a coil. "All done!" I exclaim, patting his shoulders triumphantly.

I scoot to his side and take a seat as he pulls the braid in front of his face to examine my work. "I am impressed."

"Yes, I am extremely talented," I say with a smirk. I take a sip of tea before leaning back on my elbows, taking in the glorious view in front of me.

Ahlvo mirrors me and lets out a contented sigh as he stretches out his long legs. "Tell me about your life on Earth."

I inhale deeply, and unleash the short version of my life story; including my dad's drinking problem, my mom's death, and how many jobs I had to work at one time just to pay for grad school. He listens so well, and I find myself continuing all the way up to the night my fiancé Ben cheated on me with my "best friend," Kelly, at my birthday party.

"I am confused," Ahlvo says once I'm done. "Why would your friend betray you? And why would your mate choose another?"

"I've asked myself those questions many times," I tell him as I sit up and cross my legs in front of me, my shoulders hunching despite the distance between me and those two assholes. "I think I misjudged my friend. I gave our bond more credit than it deserved." Technically, she was the "best" friend I had at the time, but only because we were neighbors, and I didn't have anyone else. She was always around, sure, but we didn't have the same intimacy and trust that real friends have.

"And as for my ex," I continue, "I didn't even cry when I caught Ben cheating. I laughed. I actually left my birthday party laughing. Apparently, I wasn't surprised." I pick up my slice of bread and start pulling it into smaller chunks. "I was so busy all the time—with school and all the side jobs I was juggling. He was someone to come home to at the end of the day. Nothing more. He wasn't the one I was supposed to end up with... I just got comfortable."

Ahlvo holds my gaze, his mouth a grim line. "He was not worthy of you. That is clear. I hope he spends all of his days cloaked in shame for how he treated you."

"Eh, it's in the past," I say dismissively as I nibble on my bread. I don't tell Ahlvo that Ben wanted kids and I didn't—I didn't even tell Ben I didn't want kids. Well, I tried early in our relationship, but he looked at me like I had just confessed to murdering a litter of kittens.

After that, anytime he brought up the subject, I lied and said that I was pumped to become a mom someday. Like, see? I'm a normal woman! Don't worry! And I think some part of me hoped I'd never have to deal with it. Ultimately, my wish came true. But Ahlvo doesn't need to get that deep into my business. We just met.

Ahlvo tilts his head, thinking. "Are Kay-teh and Cloh-ee your friends? You seem to care for them quite a lot."

My lips form an instant smile. "Yes, yes, they are. The first real friends I've had in a long time, maybe ever. Well, since my mom, anyway. It's nice to have people I can count on, especially right now."

Ahlvo's expression is filled with understanding. He nods. "Finding your clan is an invaluable gift."

I fold the empty cloth napkin and put it on the blanket next to me before lying down. "That it is," I reply.

"I should like to be your friend as well, Aye-vah, if you will let me," Ahlvo says with his big purple eyes so hopeful, it warms my insides.

"Okay. Sure," I tell him. "Friends."

Our first day in the cabin passes quickly with me unpacking our clothes into the single wooden chest. I arrange Ahlvo's medications and bandage supplies in the order he needs them and dust the heck out of every surface. Ahlvo tinkers with the tools and hums an unfamiliar song while doing so, and with his hands and eyes focused on the tiny parts, he seems in a bright mood.

It must be because he's keeping himself busy. We didn't let him fiddle with anything back in the village. Kaiva and I were worried the medications would make him too loopy or that his mood was so dark that resting was better.

Clearly, we were very, very wrong. Based on how he's been, we could've handed him a piece of rope and asked him to knot and unknot it over and over and that would've been better than letting him just lie in bed staring at the wall. His hands work perfectly fine, and as long as he keeps them busy, his thoughts remain on the task and not on his lack of mobility.

Just then, Ahlvo's head snaps up and his humming ceases. "Are you hungry?"

We've been so busy that only then do I realize we haven't eaten since the smattering of fruit and jerky we nibbled on this morning.

"I shall make us some food," Ahlvo declares as he wipes the dirt and grease from his hands on a damp rag.

"Need any help?" I ask.

His lip quirks up on one side, and his eyes run over my body from head to toe like a caress. "No. Allow me to care for you for once."

Ahlvo glides his hover seat over to the crates of food and drinks we brought along and pulls out several items. I follow and dig through the beverage crate. "At least let me handle the tea. Deal?"

"O fah," he says with mock annoyance, "you are a stubborn one, you know?"

I shoot Ahlvo the deadliest side-eye I can and then stand there, silently blinking at him.

He chuckles and nods. "I am quite aware of my shortcomings, female."

"Well, as long as you're aware of them…" I trail off as I poke at the fire and ready the kettle stand above it.

We huddle around the fire pit as Ahlvo cuts up meat and vegetables and drops them into a deep pot filled with broth. I pour our teas and prepare the bowls and spoons. Right before he pulls the pot off the fire, Ahlvo leans toward me and whispers, "And now for my special seasoning." He sprinkles a fistful of a grainy yellow spice into the broth.

Ahlvo spoons out my portion, filling it almost to the brim. After five minutes of blowing on it and nibbling on junasii bread, I gulp down a spoonful, and immediately spit it onto the fire.

"Ahhh, fuck that's spicy!" I shout, panting and waving a hand in front of my tongue.

Ahlvo's bellowing laughter fills our small room. "I thought you could handle a bit of spice, Aye-vah? All the stories about the spicy food your mother made, and you cannot handle *this*?"

"I can handle puh-lenty of spice, my friend. Believe me. The Jollof rice my mom used to make would set her coworkers' mouths ablaze, but I gobbled it down. It was a recipe passed down from my great grandmother, who grew up in Nigeria. *That*," I say, pointing to the pot, "was beyond spicy. What'd you do, crush the devil's heart into a powder?"

"I do not know who that is, but I will say, others who have tried my seasoning have had similar reactions."

"What is it made of?" I ask, moving my spoon around in the bowl, examining the tiny yellow grains floating on the surface.

He takes another bite and *mmms* with his eyes closed as the spicy liquid trickles down his throat. "It is a mixture of tukahvi root and lixa-clivo herb ground into a fine dust. Both are from Trovilia, and I always make sure to purchase more when we travel to Nu'Piix."

I smile at the fond memory he's clearly picturing and take a teeny tiny bite of the meat. I brace my tastebuds for total extinction, but I'm relieved to find that the spice on the meat is subtle.

He tilts his head at me thoughtfully and says, "The key is to avoid the broth. The spice clings to it. Stick to the solids and you will survive, I promise."

Ahlvo ignores his own advice, putting his spoon aside and pouring the remaining contents down his throat.

But he's right. I nosh on the thick cubes of meat and chopped up veggies and have the feeling back in my tongue by the end of the meal. Aside from the spicy-as-fuck broth, the meal was downright tasty, and I'm impressed that Ahlvo can cook. Somehow I figured Waldric was the only one who knew how.

"That was pretty great, Ahlvo," I tell him, trying to conceal the shock in my voice.

"Surprised, eh?" he asks. When I nod sheepishly, he explains, "When Varrek and I were on training missions together, we would spend many days in the wilds of other planets. I learned immediately that Varrek can lead, but he cannot cook. So it is something I practiced, and while I am not masterful, I can prepare a small number of meals. If I could handle that," he continues, "it was one less thing for Varrek to worry about."

"He's lucky to have you as his second-in-command," I tell him.

His chin dips, and I see a flash of sadness in his gaze. "The more I can do, the more valuable I am. Or… was."

Instinctively, I want to rush to his side and wrap my arms around him. I want to remind him how much Varrek still values him and how devastated he was when he believed his presence caused Ahlvo's illusionary dream and subsequent fall.

But I'm not sure that's what Ahlvo needs to hear right now. I know how sneaky depression can be. If I try to counter what I think are negative thoughts with positive reinforcement, will he actually hear it? Or will his depression tell him I'm just trying to make him feel better by lying to him?

I decide to change the subject.

"Let's play a game," I tell him. Getting him out of his head seems to work, so that's what I'll try when he seems lost.

He agrees, looking intrigued at my suggestion. We quickly put the dirty dishes in a bin, and I pull Ahlvo's hover seat toward me, so we're face to face. When Ahlvo lowers the control stick of his hover, there's nothing between us.

I tug on his large calloused hands and position them so his palms are facing down. Then I put my hands, palms up, underneath his, barely touching. Warmth radiates between his hands and mine and it makes me want to close the distance completely. My fingers twitch with the urge to trace every scar on his knuckles and learn their stories.

"What is this game called?" Ahlvo asks, his voice suddenly rough and throaty.

"Hmm. I honestly don't know if it has a name. We can call it *The Hand Slap Game*," I reply. "We take turns with who has their hands on top. The object is for the person on top to move their hands away before the person on the bottom can slap them."

He yanks his hands away, his face is twisting in horror. "Aye-vah, no. I will not strike you."

I laugh and pat his forearm comfortingly. "It's not a hard slap. I swear you won't hurt me."

The fact that Ahlvo is visibly disgusted at the idea of harming me, even if the touch is not painful and part of a game, is hard to ignore. Ahlvo has always been sweet and charming, but he also has a blood-thirsty side. It's a switch he turns on for battle, but the fact that this scary side of him exists remains a red flag. An appetite for violence, even when it's contained to a certain activity or location, can grow. Pair that with a series of setbacks and emotional turmoil with no support systems in place, and you've got an abuser in the making.

And honestly, part of me is waiting for that side of Ahlvo to emerge. Perhaps I'm looking for reasons to break my attraction to him, or maybe it's because I refuse to end up with anyone even slightly resembling my dad.

But this side isn't showing. Maybe I'm wrong about Ahlvo.

He narrows his eyes at me skeptically, then returns his palms to rest on top of mine. Quick as lightning, I flip my hands over and lightly slap his fingertips. "Ha! Gotcha."

For a brief moment, Ahlvo looks stunned. Then he shakes out his hands, and I see a sly smile spread across his lips.

He gets his hands in position, leans in, and with rapt determination says, "Again."

CHAPTER 11

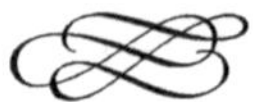

AVA

Ahlvo woke me before the sun rose and somehow convinced me to go fishing in the shallows just outside the cabin.

I blame it on his beauty. When you look like he does, you can convince anyone of anything. It's really not fair. As I'm knee deep in the water, a giggle escapes my lips as I picture him in an ill-fitting plaid blazer trying to sell cars. He'd empty the lot.

"Aye-vah," Ahlvo whispers from his hover seat on the dock a few feet away, quietly clapping his hands together to get my attention. "You must focus."

"Do fish have ears on Oluura? I don't think they can hear us," I snark in reply as I wipe the beads of sweat from my brow. I'm wearing the only fishing jumpsuit we could find in the cabin, and since it's made for a Trovilian male, it's at least six sizes too big. It's a solid beige color with waterproof boots attached at the bottom that come up to my thighs.

"They are very sensitive to vibrations and movement," he insists, tossing one of his braids over his shoulder, his voice still hushed. He quickly braided his hair this morning before we came outside, and I was blown away by how efficiently his fingers moved, weaving through the strands without even seeing them.

74

"Hey, I'm doing all the work here," I remind him, lifting my feet and sloshing in the water. It's hot inside this jumpsuit, and the humidity is only making it worse.

Since Ahlvo needs to stay off his leg, I'm the one standing in the water, placing the fish traps as the sky turns pink and purple with the dawn.

I carefully wobble to the next trap sitting on the beach and haul it into my arms. "How do these things work exactly?" I ask, examining the intricate design inside the container.

"The inner tubes are lined with small strips of jerky. That is the bait," Ahlvo says as he holds the final trap in his hands and points to each part. "The fish swim into the tubes, seeking the bait, and ultimately end up in the large enclosed section in the back. The tubes all lead there. Once the fish are in, they cannot find their way out."

"Ah, so it's like a maze. I respect the trickery," I reply with a nod. I drop the trap into the water, and it lands with a loud sloshing sound that makes Ahlvo wince and hiss.

"You must be quieter, Aye-vah," he says, shaking his head.

I place my gloved hands on my hips, my lips forming a pout. "Okay, if I'm being honest, this is not my thing, Ahlvo. I'm sorry. I really want to be a team player, but I'm sweaty and it's too damn early and it's impossible to be quiet when I'm stumbling around in this clown suit."

He sighs and crosses his arms over his chest. "Yes, you are surprisingly bad at this."

I scoff, my mouth agape. I don't care about alien fishing skills, but Ahlvo's never criticized me before. I don't like it. So I start thinking about ways I can improve, how I can move around while making less noise. Then Ahlvo throws his head back and laughs at full volume.

I stand there, waiting for him to stop, and when he finally does, he wipes tears from his eyes. "My apologies, Aye-vah. Usually, I am the one in the water, and Bruvix is yelling at me to keep quiet."

"Is that so?" I ask, kicking water in his direction. He's not close enough for me to splash him, but he puts his hands up and ducks anyway. It's satisfying.

"Besides, I am not used to seeing you do something you are not instantly skilled at. Or complain at all, for that matter," Ahlvo says, his tone tender.

"Yeah, well, I'm not used to beads of sweat rolling down the crack of my ass this early in the morning," I mutter, wading out of the water.

"Here," Ahlvo says, handing the last trap to me. "Toss this in the water near that bush on the left, and we shall check them later. We are done with this for now."

I lean back and smile at the lightening sky. "Hallelujah."

I toss the trap into the lake at the edge of the beach, and unzip my jumpsuit, climbing out of it as I walk back to the cabin. My feet are bare, but I have my regular tunic and leggings on underneath, and I'm relieved to see that the jumpsuit, while ridiculously oversized, still does its job. The sand on the beach is rough between my toes, like tiny pebbles, and I jog the rest of the way.

Once we're inside, I take a look at Ahlvo's bandages, and when I don't see any signs of swelling or blood seeping through, I decide to leave them on for another day.

Finally I climb under the furs on the bed and pass out.

* * *

When I wake, it's to the sound of rain plinking against the window. I let out a deep yawn as I stretch like a cat under the furs. My muscles feel loose, and my skin tingles with renewed energy. The sleep I've been getting at the cabin has to be the most restful sleep I've gotten in years.

I turn onto my side and frown. I'm alone. The dark purples and blues of the rainy afternoon sky cast shadows along the walls, none of which belong to my big alien roommate.

It's raining. Where could he be? I think to myself.

I climb to my feet and go to the window. It faces the back of the cabin and looks upon a grassy field. There is still no sign of Ahlvo, so I pad to the entrance and peek my head out.

The front door faces the ship, and for a moment, I wonder if he's inside, tinkering with something. Only, the interior of the ship is dark and all the doors are closed.

He must be on the dock, huddled under the awning, I conclude as my heart starts to beat faster, picking up pace with the rain. I shove my feet into my boots, throw on my cloak, and head into the rain. When I turn the corner and face the dock, I suck in a breath.

Ahlvo is on his hover seat, his back to me. He is under the awning, but it only covers about half the dock and the rain is coming down at an angle. He's drenched.

And shirtless.

The muscles in his back ripple and bunch with movement. I can't tell what he's doing, but he seems utterly unfazed by the rain.

Am I dreaming? Because I've definitely had dreams like this, of Ahlvo doing something overtly sexy, like drinking water and letting it spill down his naked chest. Or lifting a puppy in each arm and letting them use his massive biceps as pillows for their lil' puppy faces.

I step closer, trying not to disturb him or wake from this dream—if that's what this is. As I approach, I expect him to whip around and acknowledge me because he always has a way of sensing my presence, but he doesn't. When I reach his side, I notice his hands are busy, but his face is neutral and his eyes vacant. He still hasn't looked in my direction, and that worries me.

"Ahlvo? You okay?" I ask, my voice soft.

He turns his head toward me slowly and blinks a few times before saying, "Aye-vah. Hello." Then he returns to his task—gutting fish, separating the heads from the fins from the bones—on the small table from the cabin. His hands are gray with what I assume is fish blood, or guts, or both, and he is chopping up what looks to be fish fillets in the center of the table.

This is not my Ahlvo. This is the Ahlvo that would lie in bed in the med room and stare at the wall for hours without saying a word. The Ahlvo that not only lacked the smiles and laughter I've been glad to hear again, but lacked any emotion at all. I thought that tasks using his hands would help him get out of his head and quiet his depressed thoughts.

Clearly, I thought wrong.

"What are you doing out here?" I step around the table to face him.

He says nothing. It's as if he didn't hear me at all.

Part of me is disgusted by the fish guts, but this is how we survive on Oluura, so I'm learning to deal with it. My main concern is Ahlvo, his mental state, and if this is a good time for him to be holding a knife.

"Hey," I mutter, holding my hands above his, hoping he'll stop and look at me. "Let's press pause on the fish gutting, okay?"

His eyes meet mine, and they hold a heaviness that makes me want to cry. He places the knife next to the piece of fish and pushes the hover seat back from the table.

"Sorry," he says in a flat, robotic voice. Then his lips form a tight smile. "I am fine. Thank you for checking on me."

I pass him a rag from the edge of the table, and he wipes his hands. "You are not fine," I tell him, coming around to stand next to him, and bending down so I'm eye level with him. "Tell me what's happening. What's going on in that noggin of yours?"

He shakes his head dismissively, and before he can brush me off again, I say, "Please. Tell me. I might be able to help." Whenever I found him like this in the med room, I would offer to help, but he would never accept. He would remain distant, fake a few smiles, and that would be it. I don't expect this time to be any different.

Ahlvo stares at me for what feels like eternity and then tilts his head, his gaze drifting to the lake behind me. Then his chin dips and in a low voice he says, "Sometimes the fog is too loud."

"The fog?" I ask, not understanding what he's talking about. I look up to the sky, and even though it's raining, there's no fog.

He wipes his hand clean and then scratches his head, looking shy. "It is this voice in my mind. It feels like a thick, red fog. It tells me things. Makes me feel worthless."

I nod, knowingly. "And you believe what it tells you?"

"Sometimes it is hard not to."

"What makes you think it's telling you the truth?" I ask.

Ahlvo wipes at his nose and ducks his head. I crane my neck to look into his eyes, but he hides them from me. Moments before he pinches them closed, I see they're filled with unshed tears, and my heart shatters.

He's suffering so much.

"Because when I look at myself, I detect no lies," he whispers, his voice pained and thick with emotion.

I reach my hand out to take his, but before I can, he pulls away like my touch would burn him. He shakes out his shoulders and straightens his spine. Then he clears his throat and says, "I do not wish to dwell on this. I shall be fine." There is finality in his tone, and I know no amount of coaxing will get him to open up again.

I watch in thoughtful silence as he puts the fish scraps into a bucket, places the fillets in a bowl, and cleans the top of the table with a soap cube. He uses the excess soap to clean the grayness from his hands, and we silently return inside.

I place the bowl of fish fillets by the fire pit as Ahlvo glides his hover seat to the chest of clothes and grabs a dry pair of pants and a tunic. He changes in the bathroom, and when he emerges, he makes his way to where his tools are and begins fiddling with the comm cord.

"I'm going to take a bath," I tell him.

He grunts in acknowledgment but doesn't look up.

The moment I climb into the steaming hot water, I let out a long and weary exhale.

I can't do this, I think to myself. I can't want someone who shuts down the way he does. It kills me that he's in pain, and I know how evil depression can be, but I know firsthand that it's useless to help someone who doesn't want it. And if I force my help upon him, I know what'll happen… I'll become his fixer. And then I'll get sucked into a cycle of carrying all his emotional pain and watching him use unhealthy coping mechanisms. Just like my mom did with my dad.

I refuse to do that. Not only because it's unhealthy and doesn't end well for either person, but because Black women have been holding space for the emotional pain of others since the beginning of time. We have been fixers far too long.

It doesn't matter that helping people is my calling and my dream job. A job is just that and does not make up the entirety of life. At the end of a long day, I'm entitled to want a break from other people's struggles. I'm even entitled to want someone who is willing and able to hold that space for me, because I have my own struggles, and if I never leave room to face my own pain, I won't be able to help anyone else.

But... despite knowing all this, I want to be there for him. Setting aside my crush, Ahlvo is my friend and I want to support him. I want to see him through this. I just have to find a way to create a sense of balance between my instinct to take his problems from him and being there when he needs me.

The water, this tub, these moments are mine to collect my swimming thoughts, to ground myself before I face this again.

I finish scrubbing my face and body and step out of the tub. I change into my clothes and, somewhat hesitant, return to the main room. Ahlvo's still playing with the comm cord, but his head lifts, and he shoots me a warm smile.

"Um, what should we do now?" I ask, desperate for a mood shift.

Ahlvo's eyebrow lifts mischievously. "Hand Slap Game?"

"You know it."

CHAPTER 12

AHLVO

"**Y**our fingers. You have more of them. That is what gives you an advantage with the slapping game," I tell Aye-vah as she removes my bandages while kneeling at my feet. I am lying on the bed, my elbows propping me up so I can watch as she works. The morning sun beams softly through the window, and I am hoping the rain will hold off until tomorrow. We have had too many wet days during this wet season already, and it has only just begun.

Aye-vah chuckles, the sound light and melodic, causing my cock to pulse beneath my pants. "Such a sore loser. But, hey, if that's what gets you to sleep at night, keep telling yourself that, bud."

"I have not had trouble sleeping at all, actually. And I do not believe you have either," I say, steadying my gaze on her.

Her head snaps up and blood rushes to her cheeks. She looks away, suddenly shy, and continues working. There is a slight smile on her luscious lips, and I know she is thinking about last night, just as I am.

We played her slapping game before dinner, then again after dinner, and late into the night, continuing even after her eyelids grew heavy with fatigue. I did not want to stop. Partially because I lost more games than I won and was determined to beat her score, but also, because while we were playing, I could touch her. My hands would caress her slender, delicate fingers, albeit lightly, until it was either my turn or hers to flip and slap the other's. The contact steadied my mind while my insides swirled with desire.

After the slapping game, we got ready for bed and climbed under the furs, the pillow barrier still separating my side of the bed from hers. But when I awoke this morning, Aye-vah had her small hands wrapped around my bicep, her cheek pressing against my shoulder. She was all the way on my side of the bed, and the pillows that had kept us apart were scattered across the floor. I had no room to move, or breathe, but I longed to remain in that position for the rest of time.

When Aye-vah awoke and realized our night played out much like the first, she started babbling about the cold air sneaking in through a crack in the wall and how we should fix it immediately. Then she started with my bandages.

Now, Aye-vah finishes taking off my wrappings, her cheeks still flushed with pink, and stumbles toward the washroom to wash her hands and grab fresh wraps, pulling the door closed behind her.

I lie there on the bed, letting the memory of how she felt in my arms play over and over, smiling like a fool over our strengthening bond. Her body calls to mine, just as mine calls to hers. When she is asleep and her mind cannot convince her of the complications, she reaches for me. She keeps me nearby. She seeks the warmth and safety of my arms.

I am honored the goddess has blessed me with such a gift.

You are not worthy of her, and you know it, the angry fog whispers.

"O fah, you again?" I shoot back aloud. My hands ball into fists at the thought of Aye-vah witnessing my sadness yesterday. I did not expect her to find me in such a dark place. I was simply cleaning the fish freshly pulled from the traps when the fog started hurling insults at me. They came so quickly, and I could not dispute them. I let them hit me, one after the other, until my chest felt so heavy, I thought I might crumple to the ground.

"Did you say something?" Aye-vah asks as she emerges from the washroom.

I did not mean to speak aloud to the fog. "Ah, no. Nothing," I reply quickly.

Aye-vah furrows her brow, murmuring "Hmm" before shrugging it off.

She resumes her crouched position at the foot of the bed, presses the sticky edge of the bandage into my skin, and looks up at me triumphantly. "In only a few days, your leg has made incredible progress. The swelling has decreased, the blisters are shrinking, the scabs are starting to thicken, and the edges are fading to a bruise. It looks so much better."

"That is joyous news." I beam at her. Relief fills my lungs, and I let out a deep breath. I feel as if my recovery has been stagnant, and there were days when I felt like I was going backward. To finally be moving in the right direction gives me hope.

"Must be that fresh lake air," Aye-vah says as she rises and takes a seat next to me.

"Or perhaps it is you. Your healing hands are giving me precisely what I need," I tell her.

Her cheeks pinken once again, but instead of looking away, her gaze intensifies.

"As much as I would love to take credit, I think this is all you. You're finally being a not-so-terrible patient, and your body is responding," she says with a teasing grin while nudging my shoulder.

Our legs are pressed against one another, and I am so tempted to take her small hand in mine. But how will she react? Will she pull away? Will she become nervous and sputtery like she was this morning?

Of course, she will pull away, the fog adds. *You disgust her. She may not say the words, but they are present inside her mind.*

Before I can make a move, Aye-vah's eyes dart around the cabin, looking for something. "What's on the agenda for today?"

I run my fingers through my knotted mane and wince when they get caught. "I should probably bathe." I took my braids out once again before getting into bed, but there is no way I can rebraid them like this. With my leg, bathing seems to require a monumental amount of energy, strength that I simply do not possess. Even now, I do not want to go through the motions of getting myself clean, despite knowing that I need to and that I want to be clean for Aye-vah.

"Oh! Okay, yeah, let me get out of your way," Aye-vah exclaims as she stands with an eager hop. "I'll wash the dishes from last night."

I grab her before she can skip away, her eyes widen when she looks down at our clasped hands. "I may need, um…"

Her fingers lace through mine, and she bends to be eye level with me. "Tell me what you need, Ahlvo. It's okay. That's why I'm here."

She is right. I know she is right, but that does not make it any less embarrassing. "I… I might need help getting into the wash basin."

Pathetic. What kind of male cannot wash his own body? the fog points out.

I brace myself for Aye-vah to laugh at my request, to be disgusted at my show of weakness, but instead of either reaction, she smiles warmly and replies, "That I can do." Then she pats my arm and gets up from the bed. "Sit tight. I'll get the bath started for you."

Aye-vah is not known for heartless mockery, so I certainly was not expecting any, but to be an exceptionally skilled warrior one day, and the next, a sad male who cannot even maneuver his body into a tub of water, it is hard to accept. I wish more than anything that I did not need her assistance, but I have upset her in the past with attempts to do things for the sake of my pride, and I refuse to be the source of her sadness.

If I am ever given the opportunity to win her affections, I must be a source of joy. Nothing less.

My inara returns a moment later surrounded by steam from the washroom that accentuates her beguiling figure, and her full hips do that mesmerizing sway as she approaches. I put my crutch under one arm, and Aye-vah ducks her head underneath the other, helping me hobble into the washroom.

She pulls the door closed to keep the steam in, closing us in with it, a decision that flames my desperate need for her. She releases me and stands there, waiting.

"Are you, um, able to remove your pants… or…" she asks timidly.

Right. I will be naked before her, which normally would not bother me, but in this moment, my cock is straining against my pants, and I can feel precome pooling at the tip. Surely, she will know that she is the cause, yes? And how will that make her feel? Humans are not as comfortable with nudity as we are, and while Aye-vah has given me sponge baths at home, this is not the same. Those interactions were more clinical, and I was nowhere near recovery.

"If you could steady me, I will be able to remove them," I tell her.

I hear Aye-vah swallow as she nods and looks at the wall, the bath —she looks anywhere but at me. She moves to stand behind me and rests her hands lightly on either side of my ribcage, ready to catch me. Her hand presses against a tender patch of skin on my side, and a hiss escapes my gritted teeth.

"What is it?" she asks, her tone thick with concern.

I lift my arm and find a scrape along my ribcage that is starting to bruise.

"What happened here?" Aye-vah breathes.

I clench and unclench my fist in an attempt to keep my hips from jerking. Her hot breath rushing over my skin sends a jolt straight to the head of my cock. It is impossible not to imagine what that mouth would feel like around my head, licking and sucking on the tip.

"It, uh, it must be from my fall. It is fine," I say, struggling to keep my breaths from turning ragged. She will surely suspect something is wrong if that happens.

I lean my weight on my crutch as my fingers fumble with the strings at the waist of my pants. Aye-vah inhales sharply the moment they hit the floor and pool around my feet. My muscles instinctively tighten under her gaze—a gaze I can feel all over my body, even though she is behind me.

I clear my throat and whisper, "I am ready, Aye-vah," letting her name slip past my lips in a purr.

A moment passes, and then, "Sorry, sorry," she mumbles, panicked. She keeps her hands on me as she circles around my body until we are face to face. Her eyes are pinched shut and her brow is furrowed. I would give anything to lean over and nudge that brow with my nose to smooth it. Aye-vah does not wish to make me uncomfortable. She does not realize that I am wholly hers, and she is entitled to an eyeful whenever she wishes.

I reach out and lightly trace her jawline with my thumb. "It might be better to keep your eyes open while helping me into the wash basin. I would prefer it, actually."

Her eyes pop open, and when she smiles, my heart feels as if it will explode out of my chest. I will never tire of seeing those blunt little teeth when she is happy. Or the crinkles by her eyes and corners of her mouth when a grin stretches across her face. She keeps her rich brown eyes focused on mine, almost as if she is afraid they will dip to my cock if she dares to break her gaze. It is pulsing for her, standing at attention between us, practically reaching for her.

"Um, wh–what can I do?" Aye-vah asks.

I lean over the basin and drop my crutch on the floor next to it. "If you could hold my bad leg and keep it above the water until I climb in, I am capable of handling the rest."

"Sure thing!" she exclaims, seemingly grateful to have a specific task to distract her from my nakedness.

I brace my left hand on the curved edge of the stone basin and carefully step my good leg into the water while swinging my injured leg above the surface. The bandages are fine to get wet, but I prefer to submerge my torn flesh into the hot water slowly. Aye-vah places her hands beneath my calf, holding my wounded leg parallel above the water.

Once I am fully seated and under the water, Aye-vah lowers my leg beneath the surface, allowing me time to get used to the temperature. Her eyes remain locked on my body and I hear her breaths turn shallow. I dip my arms under the surface and rub the muscles of each leg until they begin to loosen, watching her heated gaze as it follows the path of my hands.

Aye-vah stands and asks in the quietest voice, "Do you need anything else?"

"No," I tell her. "I am able to do the rest. If you could come back when I finish, however..."

"Of course. Just, um, give me a shout," she says in a flustered, husky voice before exiting the steam-filled room and closing the door behind her.

Once my legs are fully massaged, I use the soap cubes to wash my body and then my mane, gently working out the knots as I run my fingers through it. Surprisingly, it has been nice to have my braids out at night, allowing my mane to hang free. My scalp does not feel as tight.

The water turns cool, and once my body is completely clean, I call Aye-vah's name.

She strides in with a determined look on her face and a towel in her hand. This is the Aye-vah from the village. The healer. The female who assists my mother. This is not my inara, who, only moments ago, had such a fierce look of desire on her face that it seemed like she wanted to devour me.

I lift out of the water, and she circles me, propping my crutch under my left arm and putting my right arm across her shoulders. Once I am standing, she wraps the towel around my hips while her head is turned away. "Can you hang tight for a sec while I grab you another towel for your hair?" she asks.

"Yes," I let out, only managing a rasp.

She returns and tucks each dripping lock of my mane into the towel as she rubs and scrunches and presses the water out of it. A relaxed groan escapes my lips as she continues her ministrations, and she freezes at the sound before setting the towel across my shoulders. "Okay," she says as she grabs my pants from the floor, "ready?"

"I am," I reply, trying not to let the citrusy scent of her mane make me dizzy.

My fingers lightly grip her shoulder as she helps me hop away from the basin and to the bed. As she tosses my pants across the foot of the bed, her hip bumps against mine…

We tumble, a mess of legs and arms on top of the furs. We land on our sides, nose to nose, and clutching each other tightly. Aye-vah looks down at my leg with alarm and gasps. "Oh my god! Are you okay? I'm so sorry!"

"It is okay. My leg is no worse than before," I tell her. Falling onto my left side protected my bad leg from bending or stretching the wrong way.

She releases a sigh mixed with a giggle. "Thank the goddess. I never would've forgiven myself if I made your injury worse."

I reach up and lightly brush an errant curl from her forehead. "You could never do that. Day after day, you make me better."

Her gaze drops from my eyes to my lips, and back up again, then she crushes her mouth to mine.

At first, her lips are soft, tender. And almost immediately, they become frenzied. They open against mine, and I groan when her little tongue swipes against the seam of my mouth. I let her in as I pull her body closer, until she is completely pressed against me, from her shoulders to her toes. My hands clutch her back. A soft moan slips from her lips, and I respond by swirling my tongue against hers as I reach down to grip one of the fleshy globes of her ass, reveling in the way it is too much for my hand to hold.

Aye-vah writhes against me, and I feel her nipples harden under her tunic as they rub against my bare skin. How long I have waited for this. To hold her. To taste her. And it far exceeds every one of my fantasies. Her scent fills my nose, and the way it blends with the sweetness of her taste, it makes me want to drink her down and inhale her at the same time.

She is exquisite, this creature in my arms, and I am desperate to make her come. It feels as if there has never been a mission more important in the entirety of my existence. My soul needs her to moan my name, to tear at my skin with her little nails, and to give her body so much pleasure that she shakes with the intensity of it for hours on end.

There is nothing but Aye-vah.

Her hands go to my mane as our tongues dance. I wrap my hand around the nape of her neck, pulling her closer to me. Her hand slips from my mane and travels down the side of my face, reaching my neck, then my chest, my stomach... And just as her fingers reach the top of the towel at my waist—

She jerks back, putting distance between our bodies.

We lay there, still on our sides, our chests heaving as we gasp for breath. Fear and uncertainty have risen in her eyes, and I am worried I have done something to put it there.

"What is it?" I ask, lightly skimming her forearm in a comforting gesture. "Tell me."

She blinks at me for what feels like an excruciatingly long time before she swallows and says, "I-I'm sorry."

"Why are you sorry?" I ask, aghast at this sudden change in mood. "We do not have anything to apologize for."

She sits up and scoots to the edge of the bed. She grabs my pants, fiddling with the string at the waist, saying nothing.

Did I scare her? Was I too rough with her?

She turns to face me, her eyes not meeting mine, and hands me my pants. "I'm going to wash those dishes before the food gets stuck there forever. You can, uh, put these on yourself?"

I take the pants from her, stunned, confused, and deeply frustrated. "I can."

"Great. Be back in a few."

I sit up, remove my towel, and begin to tug my pants on. "*Great*?" I mumble to myself. That is the last word I would choose for this moment.

CHAPTER 13

AVA

tupid, stupid, stupid!

I continue to berate myself as I scrub the dishes from last night's dinner. I'm honestly surprised the bowl in my hands hasn't shattered under my white-knuckled grip. I'm crouched beneath the thin cloth awning on the side of the cabin, using the outdoor spigot. Goose bumps cover my arms as the rain starts to fall. Again. I didn't realize the "wet season" was going to be so damn wet.

Thanks to the awning, the rain isn't hitting me directly, but if the wind picks up at all, I'm going to get drenched out here. Truthfully, a cold shower is exactly what I need. My pussy is still throbbing at the memory of that kiss.

Why did I pull away? What the hell is wrong with me? I finally got the courage to kiss Ahlvo, something I've been daydreaming about since the day I met him, and I pulled away when things got intense. My hand was hovering over the top of his towel, seconds away from unwrapping his superhero body like a present on Christmas morning, and I chickened out.

I knew the kiss would be good, but I never expected it to be *that* good. The way his strong hands gripped my ass. The way his mouth knew exactly how I wanted to be kissed. The way his pupils expanded to the point where his eyes were completely black. The way his hold on the back of my neck felt primal and dominant, but not too rough. How does he know what turns me on when we've never hooked up? Is it because he's experienced in bed? Or are we just sexually compatible?

Stop thinking about how scorching hot the sex would be, I tell myself.

I can't make this mistake again. We can't be pleasure mates. As I keep telling myself: one day, he's going to find his mate, and that will crush me. I cannot watch him fall in love with someone else. Sure, we could have a little fun before that day comes, but in the back of my mind I'd always know that his mate is lurking around the corner about to take him from me. I wouldn't be able to enjoy it knowing I will eventually lose him.

Besides, he's my patient, I reason. *It would be unprofessional to have a relationship with him.*

He's also severely depressed and has trouble opening up.

Plus, he might have a drinking problem.

And technically, his mother is my boss which would make things awkward.

Not that the clan, or even Kaiva, would care if we became pleasure mates. I'm almost certain they don't have any restrictive rules on romance.

So… am I coming up with reasons to extinguish my feelings before they grow any stronger? Yes.

Is this strategy actually going to work? Probably not.

Because I'm afraid I'm already in too deep. Just a taste of him makes me want more, and I'm not sure "more" will ever be enough when it comes to Ahlvo.

I put the dry bowls on the wooden porch and reach for the pot. I pour water in and drop in a soap cube. Then I scrub. I scrub and I scrub and let the repetitive motion distract me. It works temporarily.

The rain is now falling in fat droplets and my clothes are getting sprinkled with the splash of each one. I need to finish this soon and get back indoors. I rinse the pot and quickly clean the utensils before tossing them with the other clean dishes.

Once inside, I find Ahlvo is cleaning the comm cord, but when I toe off my boots by the door, his head pops up and he offers me a hesitant smile.

"Raining again," I mutter, putting the dish bin next to the fire pit.

"It is that time of year," Ahlvo replies flatly, brushing his neatly braided hair out of his face and over his shoulder.

Small talk about the weather—is that where we are now? Ugh, I really don't want things to be weird between us, and I have no idea how to fix the mess I caused.

CHAPTER 14

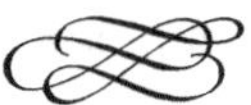

AHLVO

Aye-vah is uncomfortable. That much is obvious. She kissed me and then ran outside to get away from me. Now that it is raining, she is stuck inside. With me.

She kneels next to the fire pit, stacking the clean dishes she just washed. It's work that doesn't need to be done, and I know it is a nervous behavior. I watch her from my hover seat in the far corner of the room, surrounded by my tools, feeling helpless and discouraged.

I do not know how to comfort her in this moment, and that makes my chest ache. My useless instincts tell me to do what any male would do for his inara: wrap her in my arms and tell her everything will be okay. But she pulled away from my physical touch not even an hour ago, so that is a terrible idea.

Clearly, she regrets kissing you. You did not do it right. Or she found your breath revolting. Perhaps both are true, which would not be surprising because you ruin everything, the angry fog sneers. *She wants you to leave. Go out in the rain. It does not matter if you get wet. Make her happy and get away from her.*

I glance at Aye-vah, look out the window, and decide to listen to the fog. Aye-vah desires space from me, so that is what I shall give her, even if it is only for a little while.

"I am going to check the wiring outside," I tell her, dropping my tools on the floor and guiding my hover seat to the door.

"Ahlvo, it's pouring out," Aye-vah reminds me.

I nod. "I know. It is okay. I do not mind the rain."

"Um, okay." She nibbles on the inside of her cheek. "Do you have to check the wiring now? Can't it wait until later or something?"

I shake my head, making this task seem much more urgent than it is. "We do not know when the rain will stop, and if the wiring outside is damaged, we will not be able to set up the comm line at all. I should have checked it the moment we arrived."

"Oh," Aye-vah says as she looks out the window at the falling rain. "Do you need any help?"

"No. I will not be gone long," I vow.

Aye-vah nods in acceptance and steps aside so I can reach the door.

I smile at her as I pass, and she offers me one in return. It feels forced.

As the door closes behind me, I grit my teeth and curse the angry fog for coaxing me out here.

But now Aye-vah is happy. You want her to be happy, do you not? it asks.

I do. Of course, I do. I would cut my limbs from my body with a rusty blade if it would make Aye-vah happy.

I glide the hover seat around the house to the back where the wires are located as thick raindrops land on my head and arms. I know there is nothing wrong with the wires—they are secured together with multiple ties and protected from the elements with a sealed adhesive— but just in case Aye-vah watches me from the window, I will pretend to check the wires.

I make a show of leaning over the side of my hover seat to inspect the ties, looking closely, and nodding in approval. Then I drop the wires and lean back for a moment, poking my plated brow with my finger as if lost in deep contemplation.

My act is interrupted when I hear a muffled cry over my shoulder. I turn toward it, facing where the beach cuts inward and is covered with thin and wiry gray bushes. I glide over, following the sound. It is a noise I have heard before, but I am having trouble placing it.

Moving around the bushes, I reach the mouth of a stream that divides the sand from the darker soil on the other side, leading into a long stretch of tall grass. I let my ears guide me and stop where the sound is loudest in front of a bush. Peeling back the stiff branches, I find a small puuwaba bird chirping and screeching in pain. Looking closer, I notice that one of its four feet is tangled in the roots of the bush. From its size, I reckon it is a baby.

The puuwaba appear to be local to the lake as we have not seen them in the village, but they have been pleasant to watch. This bird hunts small fish that swim close to the surface of the water, and Varrek and I have spent many hours cheering on the puuwaba from the dock, congratulating those who emerge from the lake with a fish dangling from their small green beaks. They are covered in black, oily feathers, and have large white eyes.

The puuwaba do not appear to be aggressive, so I do not hesitate to reach down and free the baby bird's foot from the roots. The moment it is freed, it hops up and down a few times, testing the health of its foot.

But while it lifts its wings, it does not fly. I do not see any obvious injuries and would not know what to do even if I did. But I gently reach down and clasp my hands around the puuwaba, bringing it to my chest.

It has ceased its screeching, which I take to be a good sign. Perhaps it just needs to be reunited with its family. I am sure I can manage that.

"Come, tiny one," I whisper to it.

I shift the bird into my left hand as I use my right to pull my tunic over my head. I place the bird onto the fabric and slowly wrap the excess cloth around it, keeping it warm. I am not sure if this bird is able to detect cold temperatures, but I figure warmth cannot hurt, even if it is purely for comfort. It seems to snuggle into it.

I place the bundled puuwaba in my lap and begin the search for its family. The rain has lightened a bit, making it easier to scan the area. I glide farther across the sand side of the stream, and a few moments later, I find them.

I hear them first and locate them shortly after. A full-grown puuwaba, which I assume to be the mother, is screeching from the other side of the stream while safely tucked under the leaves of a young tree. Not far from the mother puuwaba are three babies the size of the one nestled inside my tunic. I lift my hover seat as high as it can go, and fly over the stream, landing far enough away from the puuwaba family to not scare them even when they notice my presence. Then I place my tunic on the wet ground next to me, and slowly unravel it so the little puuwaba can waddle free.

It hops out clumsily, screeching and chirping. "Return to your clan, little friend."

Once it lands on the soil, I retrieve my tunic, wipe off the mud, and glide back to the other side of the stream and toward the house. I look over my shoulder before I get too far away and smile as the mother puuwaba reaches the baby, poking it with its beak as the baby continues to wail.

I pull my tunic over my head before I reach the front door and shake the water out of my braids.

Aye-vah's eyes find mine as I enter, a surprisingly warm smile lighting up her face. I am relieved that was an adequate amount of time to give her space because the rain has chilled me to the bone and I do not plan on going back outside anytime soon.

CHAPTER 15

AVA

I zip around the house, quickly toweling off my rain-soaked hair and changing into a dry shirt, desperate to appear like I've been here the whole time. Ahlvo will be back soon. I look around, searching for busy work. I hear the low mechanical hum of his hover seat and know the front door will swing open within seconds. I'm out of time.

I crouch in front of the boxes of food and drink rations and start moving them around inside their containers, pretending to do… something.

He doesn't need to know I followed him outside.

At first, I had no intention of doing it, but he was acting so weird, and I couldn't just sit here and wait for him to come back. I knew there was no rush to check the wires, so I assumed it was an excuse to get away from me. And that's fair. Our kiss has turned me into an awkward wreck.

But part of me wanted to discover that he lied. Maybe he wouldn't check the wires at all but sneak sips of alcohol behind my back. Or something. I wanted another item to add to my "con" list, and what I got was the exact opposite.

Not only did he actually check the wires, but then I watched him rescue a baby bird and return it to its family. He saved a cute, helpless, injured animal, used the shirt off his back to keep it warm, and then he returned it to its mother. The worst part? He did all of this in the pouring rain.

If I could successfully kick my own ass, I would.

I pulled away from the lips of a man who saves baby birds. A man who has made me feel safe when lost in space. A man who has made me laugh in times of extreme panic. And here we are, alone in this little lake house, and I'm spending my time searching for reasons not to be attracted to him?

Before I can slam my face into my palm, the front door opens with a low creak, and in comes Ahlvo, drenched and muddy. He glides in on his hover seat, wringing out the wet ends of his hair.

"Ah, the goddess is giving us a relentless wet season, it seems," Ahlvo says with a chuckle.

I hand him a towel and a dry shirt, and he gives me a grateful nod as he dries his braids. The moment he pulls his shirt over his head, I force my gaze to turn away—I can't see that perfect chest right now. If I do, I'm pretty sure I'll drop to my knees before him with my mouth open, begging him to put his giant golden dick into my mouth.

Instead, I decide to distract myself with chores. There's nothing sexy about cleaning the bathroom, so I hurry in there and close the folding door behind me. Did it look like I was having a bathroom emergency? Possibly, but whatever. Maybe that'll take the sexual tension down a few pegs.

* * *

The sun sets later that day, and it's still raining. I've cleaned the bathroom, I've taken a bath, I've organized the food—first by freshness and then by size—and I've covered the small holes in the walls with fabric scraps and tape.

But it's not enough. I'm still very much tempted to put my mouth on Ahlvo's mouth. I guess I could wash our clothes, or maybe organize the remaining medical supplies, alphabetically this time…

Ahlvo interrupts my thoughts. "Fanu cihlox ke," he growls at the cord in his hands which translates to "pesky monk slug."

Perplexed, I make my way over to him. "Anything I can do?"

He looks up at me with tired eyes and sighs. "Ah, it is just this wretched insulation adhesive. It is supposed to last many years, but it is not sticking the way I need it to."

I eye his work, wondering what he's trying to accomplish.

"I am using it to protect the interior wires that are now exposed," Ahlvo says, showing me how the adhesive forms like clay outside the wires. It stretches and molds under his big, beautiful hands, but when he goes to close the edges together, it slowly flops back open.

Then a happy memory pops into my mind. "Paste! I could make a paste," I suggest, excitedly.

"Paste? This is an adhesive from Earth?" he asks, his brow scrunching as I nod. "How would you make this paste?"

"Well, all I need is flour and water, and I know the flour here is different, but it should work," I say, second-guessing my suggestion already. The last thing I want to do is disappoint Ahlvo twice in one day. "Maybe it won't work, but it's worth a try."

I grab a bowl, dig for the small bag of flour, and take a seat at the table next to the spigot. I mix the ingredients, adding a pinch of the Oluuran equivalent to salt to prevent mold from forming, and swirl my spoon in a rapid motion until the lumps disappear.

When I take the bowl to Ahlvo, he stares at it for a full minute before dipping his finger in and licking off the paste.

"Ahlvo!" I yell, shoving his shoulder playfully. Despite everything, I laugh, and hope fills my chest at the prospect of us moving past the earlier weirdness.

"Well, I am glad that this is paste, because it does not taste very good," he says with a teasing grin.

He dips his finger in again, and this time, adds a light coat to the seam of the adhesive clay.

"Maybe add a few coats. It will take a few minutes to dry," I point out, silently praying that it works.

I watch his tongue dart out as he licks his lips, exposing the sharp point of his fang. He gently blows on the drying paste, and my insides melt. I want that mouth on me. On my mouth, my neck, my nipples… everywhere.

I swallow the tension, waiting for the paste to dry, trying really hard *not* to picture Ahlvo using those fangs to bite into my neck as I grip his shoulders and ride out wave after wave of orgasms. I've never been into biting, really, but seeing Ahlvo's fangs makes me want his mark on my skin. To know that I'm his.

"It appears to have worked. Brilliant, Aye-vah!" Ahlvo cheers, pausing my heated thoughts. I was so distracted I hadn't noticed.

"Woohoo!" I shout with glee.

"There are several spots on the cord that have exposed wires. Can you help me?" he asks.

"Of course."

After successfully patching up a third section of the wire cover, Ahlvo shoots me a thoughtful glance. "How did you learn this?" he asks.

Usually when memories of my mom pop into my head, I push them away before the weight of her death crushes me. But this time, I let them settle. "When I was in elementary school, my class had to put on a play for the entire school about a holiday we call Thanksgiving. My teacher wanted me to wear this costume… it was awful. Incredibly offensive. He thought it was a good way to "honor" the history behind the holiday, but it wasn't. Anyway, I refused to wear it and got detention for two weeks."

I pause, deciding some context is needed. "Detention is a form of punishment."

Ahlvo stops me, his violet eyes bright with curiosity. "And you chose not to wear this costume because it would be hurtful to others?"

"Yes. History matters, and framing it incorrectly has dire consequences," I reply.

"You are right," Ahlvo says with a thoughtful nod. "Ignoring the truth of past atrocities only creates more pain, usually for those who have already suffered too much."

A smile tugs at the corners of my lips. Of course, he understands. "I came home crying and told my mom what happened. She was pissed but not surprised, and wrapped me up in the biggest, tightest hug," I say, closing my eyes as I breathe in the phantom scent of her coconut shampoo. "She left the room to call the school and report my teacher, and when she came back, she said, 'Let's make something.'

"She showed me how to create this paste, we gathered every scrap of paper we could find in the house, and we made these pretty red bowls covered with flowers. When we were done, she asked, 'How do you feel when you look at this?' and when I told her it made me happy, she said, 'I can't change how the world treats you, baby girl. If I had that power, I would crush anyone who caused you pain. But when you look at this bowl, I want you to remember that in the face of evil, you have the ability to create something truly beautiful. That is a gift. And no one can take that from you.'"

Tears threaten to spill onto my cheeks, and I clench my fists to hold them back. "It certainly wasn't the last time I came home crying from school. But each time, my mom broke out the paper, we made the paste, and we created something cool together. Dozens of times, the world showed how cruel it could be. Dozens of times, I created more pretty things with that paste: paper lanterns, teacups, animal figurines, plant holders, and holiday decorations. It always made me feel better." I swallow the lump in my throat. "Still does."

I look down and realize that Ahlvo is holding my hand. I have no idea how long we've been like this, but I know I don't want him to let go, even if both of our hands are covered in paste.

Ahlvo clears his throat. "Your mother seems like she had a heart as big as the sun. You were as lucky to have her as she was to have you."

"Thank you," I murmur, his kind words tugging my gaze to his mouth.

I can't keep doing this. I need to either pounce on him or pour some cold water on this whole situation. Metaphorically speaking. The latter would probably be best for both of us, right? But I don't know how to do that. Should I just start talking about something incredibly dull? Maybe explain the rules of golf?

You don't know the rules of golf, I remind myself.

Or should I be direct and bring up the elephant in the room? Explain that the kiss was a moment of weakness and why we can't go any farther because we're not mates? In the entire world of subjects to discuss, I can't think of anything but golf and our kiss.

"Ahlvo, listen, about that kiss earlier…" I begin. "I'm really sorr—"

"No, Aye-vah, I am sorry," he interrupts. He lets go of my hand and hangs his head. "I did not mean to push you."

"Oh, no. You didn't push. That was all me. It was just…" I pause, trying to come up with the right words to describe it. "I was caught up in the moment, I guess. But clearly, it would be a bad idea to do that again."

Ahlvo stares at me thoughtfully. "It would?"

"I mean, yeah. For one, I work for your mom," I reason, counting off with my fingers. "And two, you're technically my patient, which would cross all kinds of ethical lines on Earth."

"I do not think your Earth rules apply here," he says, his tone calm and rational.

"Well, it's not only that," I say. "Look," the truth is bubbling up my throat, and maybe it's because I'm already in a vulnerable state after sharing the memory of my mom, or the way Ahlvo held my hand as I told it, but I feel like I can't keep this in any longer. "If you and I become pleasure mates, which I would be totally on board with, by the way," I blink, gulp, and continue, "it would crush me to lose you, you know, when you finally meet your inara."

Ahlvo's mouth hangs open, but he says nothing, so I continue. "Don't get me wrong, I would be thrilled for you. So, so, happy. You're my friend, and I want you to find your mate. I just… okay, fine!" I shout, throwing my hands up in defeat. "I'm into you. I think I've been into you since the first day we met. And being your pleasure mate wouldn't be enough, not for me. I want all of you. I've never felt this way about anyone before. So I guess, I'm falling in love with you. But I also know that I'm not your inara. I know that. And it's okay, really."

I pause to take a breath. What have I done? Now that Ahlvo knows how I feel, we can never go back to being buddies. "I will always support you and be there for you. Just know that when I kissed you, I felt it: the magic. The stuff you're supposed to feel. Does that make sense? Ugh, this is all starting to sound like a cheesy pop song."

Ahlvo perks up and opens his mouth as if to say something, but I stop him. I don't want to lose this momentum, and I'm also not ready to face the sting of rejection. "I know things are different between us now, and I'm sorry. But this will absolutely not change my role as your healer. I will be by your side every step of the way until you're fully recovered… assuming you still want me."

Ahlvo blinks. He wrings his hands together as his gaze darts across the floor. He looks worried, and that makes me brace even harder. If he goes with the whole "it's not you, it's me," thing, I swear I'm going to walk straight into the lake.

"Aye-vah, I… I wish that I—" he starts, but I hold up a hand to stop him.

I know what he's going to say, and I can't take it. My skin feels itchy, and I want to scratch it all off. My breaths are coming out in rapid, short puffs, and I feel my heartbeat pulsing intensely behind my eyes.

"It's okay, Ahlvo, really," I say. "I need to get some air. I'll be right back, okay? 'K, great. Thanks," I mutter as I rush outside, slamming the door shut behind me.

CHAPTER 16

AVA

"Well, at least it's not raining," I say with a sardonic chuckle, my feet stomping through the thick sand on the beach as I march along, huffing. There's a chill in the air, and I hug my arms around my waist to keep warm. The purple sky is getting darker by the minute, and when my stomach growls, I realize it's dinner time.

Fuck.

The last thing I want to do is have an unbearably tense dinner with Ahlvo and wade through the long stretches of silence hanging between us.

But I also can't stay out here forever. I'm not even sure why I'm still out here. Why delay the inevitable?

I mean, I know why. I don't want him to break my heart. This might be the first time I've acknowledged that Ahlvo has the ability *to* break my heart. It's belonged to him for a while. And now he's aware of the power he holds.

The wet sand is squishy beneath my boots, and I kick at it as I pace. I'm only fifteen feet from the cabin, and I can't seem to step any closer. Since it's been raining the whole time we've been here, I haven't explored this part of Oluura, and I have no idea what kinds of predators lurk along the waterfront at night. Plus, ever since Chloe was kidnapped from the village, I know that animals aren't the only ones who see us as prey.

So, I walk back and forth on this short strip of sand next to the dock, chiding myself for telling him the truth while I form a deep groove in the beach with my aggressive pacing. Part of me does feel relieved—now it's all out in the open—but it's hard to enjoy it with the crippling fear that has taken its place. I have no idea how long it will take Ahlvo to recover or when he'll be healed enough to return to the village. Until that day comes, it's just the two of us, sharing a very small cabin. And a bed.

How am I supposed to sleep next to him now? My traitorous body has sought him out every single night since we arrived. It's been magnificent, sure, but he'll most likely want to put a stop to that now that he knows I'm crushing hard on him.

I guess I could sleep on the floor. We have enough blankets that I could create a makeshift mattress.

I think of my bed back in the village and sigh. I miss that bed. I miss the sun shining into my window through the trees, waking me each day. I miss going to the food hall with the girls, piling our plates high with sweet bread and berries, not worrying about portions or rationing each meal to make it last. I even miss morning dish duty. It was my only chance to see the entire clan, and I loved saying hi to everyone as they handed over their plates and bowls to be cleaned.

I miss spending the day with Kaiva, learning from such a supportive and generous healer. She's exactly the type of mentor I hoped to find when I planned to become a therapist. I never expected to make this kind of monumental career shift, but it's been wonderful. Kaiva is always happy to answer my questions no matter how stupid or basic I think they are. She's eager to hear about the differences between human medicine and theirs. And she's patient when I have trouble grasping a certain technique.

Thinking about Kaiva naturally makes me think about Ahlvo, and I spare a glance at the cabin. He hasn't followed me out here, and I'm not sure how to take that. It seems like a bad sign, since in every rom-com the guy always runs after the girl. I know Ahlvo can't exactly run after me, but he could fly his hover seat out here to check on me at least, right?

Maybe he's giving me the space I need. I mean, there's really no need to rush out here just to reject me.

Instead of fixating on what will happen once I go back inside, I let my mind drift. I fantasize about Ahlvo rushing outside, concerned that I've wandered too far, and professing his love for me as the rain starts to fall. I run toward him, my clothes soaking wet, and he picks me up, drapes me across his lap on his hover seat, and we make out like we're the last two people on this planet, on all the planets, until the rain stops.

I'm closing my eyes, allowing the image of him tugging on my bottom lip with his fang play out when I hear a crunch under my foot.

The hell?

When I look down, I see the jagged, broken edges of what looks like a large shell about the size of a softball. It's a dull gray color, and I'm terrified to lift my boot and see what I've crushed. It must've been buried deep beneath the sand, and my angry sand-kicking uncovered it.

Holding my breath, I slowly lift the toe of my boot and find a smaller, darker gray shell that appears unscathed.

"Whew," I mutter with an exhale.

I lean down and inspect the uncracked inner shell a bit closer. Should I move it? Should I bury it under the sand even deeper to protect whatever is inside?

Pausing on that last thought, I wonder if the thing inside is a blood-sucking insect or a giant alien spider, and my body trembles. Bugs are absolutely *not* my thing.

The sight of blood? No biggie.

Heights? Pfft. Take me to the tallest building.

Public speaking? Meh. Don't hate it, don't love it.

Snakes? I could do without the hissing, but otherwise, I don't mind them.

But bugs? Hard pass. Burn it down. Get me the fuck outta here.

I'm more of an indoorsy type of gal and the prospect of having to tango with weird flies or creepy crawlies has kept me from camping, hiking, picnicking, and traveling to Australia.

If there's a way to enjoy the day sans bugs, I will always choose that option.

My hand hovers over the delicate shell, my fear of bugs warring with my instinct to help other living creatures.

I quickly dig a hole about a foot away from where the shell is so I can pick it up, gently drop it in, and cover it with sand before whatever is inside can crawl out.

Pinching my eyes closed, I suck in a breath and hold it.

I gingerly wrap my fingers around the edges of the shell, and just as I begin to lift, the top half crumples in on itself. I drop the flaky broken edges, horrified.

A swarm of red, centipede-like bugs with wiggly bodies, too many feet, and matching red wings fly out of the shell. They form a cloud of high-pitched trills around my head.

I can't really see them; there are too many.

I choke out a scream, and one flies into my mouth. A muffled cry escapes me as I stomp my feet, no longer caring if I crush the shell under my boot. I cough and spit and hold one hand in front of my face as I use the other to frantically scrape at my tongue to get it out.

Eventually, I succeed.

I keep my mouth closed and throw my hands up around my head in an attempt to bat them away, but that only seems to anger them, because the swarm is now closing in on me, the chirping invading my ears. I squeal with my mouth closed, shoulders tightening.

I run. My boots dig deep into the wet sand as I push myself away from the freaky flies and toward the cabin. When I glance back to see if they're following me, the toe of my boot catches on something.

Suddenly I pitch forward, my arms are flailing as the edge of the dock rises to meet me.

I feel a hard surface beneath my head, but I can't tell what it is. I roll over into dirt. The world spins, and I hear a muffled shout as darkness closes in all around me.

CHAPTER 17

AHLVO

In the last day, Aye-vah has only opened her eyes long enough for me to feed her water and broth. She has not awakened enough for me to share my heart with her.

This could also be due to the pain medicine I have given her for the massive bump on her forehead. I do not want her mind to be fuzzy with drugs when I finally tell her the truth. I have waited so long for this moment, hoping it would come but assuming it never would, and I want to do it right.

She sleeps now, her eyes darting around rapidly beneath her shiny eyelids. I wish more than anything in this universe that she would wake. Mostly so I can confirm that her head injury did not leave lasting damage, but also, so I can tell her all the words I have kept hidden away since the day we met.

I should have interrupted her. I should have grabbed her and made her listen as I told her that she *is* my inara and there will never be another female I care for in this way. Instead, I said nothing, clearly making her think her love was not returned, and she stormed out angry and embarrassed.

She must have been distracted by those emotions when she did whatever it was to enrage the docile riahpu flies. Her mind was elsewhere when she fell and hit her head. And when she screamed, I felt as if my stomach was being shredded from the inside. The bone-shaking terror I experienced in that moment has only occurred a few times in my life.

When I was a young boy, I witnessed my father get into a fight with one of King Muryk's castle guards, one who had come into our village drunk and began mocking an elderly blacksmith with a stutter. Pride surged inside my chest as I watched my father use his strength to defend someone vulnerable. It felt right. Acceptable. Like it was the only appropriate scenario to use violence outside of war.

My father won the fight, breaking the guard's arm, but he walked away bloodied and bruised. It was my first time witnessing any kind of physical violence, and I remember how my heart lodged in my throat whenever the guard's fist connected with my father's body. How afraid I was that he would not come home with us that eve.

The second time was many years later during one of my first battles as a Trovilian warrior. We were on the planet of Gxekai II facing off against the Lloptahlo army, a despicable bunch of colonizers with orange skin who sport layers of sharp teeth in their mouths along with tongues that split into several squirmy, venomous sections and attach to the skin of their prey to suck their blood.

They look scarier than they are, mostly because they are not skilled fighters. But on this day, a Lloptahlo warrior got the upper hand and knocked my sword from my grasp. He pinned me down and held the rusted tip of his blade to my neck, and I felt that fear deep within my body that this was the end.

A heartbeat later, the Lloptahlo's head was cleanly separated from his body, landing between my legs with his single yellow eye still open. When I looked up, Varrek was there, tossing me my sword and giving me a single nod. I knew in that moment what an incredible leader he would be, and how honored I would be to stand at his side as his second-in-command.

The third time was after the virus hit Trovilia, and our females started dying in large numbers. My mother, eternally selfless, tended to the sick every moment she could. She was exhausted and putting herself at risk of contracting the virus, but she refused to abandon her duty as healer out of fear.

I do not know how many times I prayed to the goddess to keep my mother safe, but it felt as if I held my breath from the moment my mother left the house in the morning until the moment she returned from the sick ward each eve. Amazingly, my mother was spared.

These traumatic experiences have stuck with me. All resurfacing and yet incomparable to the visceral fright that shot down my spine when I heard Aye-vah shriek. I felt it in each strand of my mane. I felt it in my fingertips, my toes. I felt her terror as if it were my own. Had I not been close enough to hear her cry for help, I am certain I would have felt the jolt of fear regardless.

Responding, I slammed down on the acceleration pedal on my hover seat, flying as fast as it would allow. I busted through the front door, knocking the hinges clean off, but that would not slow my pace. I reached her unconscious form lying in the sand on the other side of the dock. Her arms were covered in swollen red welts, and blood dripped down the log beneath her head. I scooped her into my arms, and carefully minding her injuries, raced the hover seat back into the cabin. My only thought was *get to Aye-vah. Save your mate.*

Her soft groans bring me back to the present. "I'm sorry, Bee-yawn-say," she mumbles quietly. "Please forgive me."

This "Bee-yawn-say" person has been mentioned multiple times during Aye-vah's sleep, and my teeth grind together at the possibility of it being a former pleasure mate of hers. I do not think this is the name of her former mate who betrayed her. Perhaps someone else. Does she still love this Bee-yawn-say? My fists ball, my knuckles white, and upon noticing them, I attempt to calm myself.

She is exquisite. Of course, she has former pleasure mates. She probably cares more for this Bee-yawn-say than she could ever care for you. While the angry fog has been quieter since Aye-vah's injury, it has not disappeared completely. Even a declaration of love from my inara is not enough to silence it.

The fire crackles loudly, and I push the logs around with the steel poker. Then I move my hover seat to where Aye-vah has stored the salves and bandages for my leg. I grab the salve and glide over to Aye-vah's bedside. Once I've wiped the dried salve from her arms with a damp towel, I reapply it to each of her riahpu bites. There are so many, but they have gotten smaller with the help of the salve. I am sure they are itchy and hope they are gone before she fully awakens. I do not want her to experience another moment of discomfort. I hate that she has felt this much already.

As it is, that large red bump on her angelic face will haunt me for the rest of my days. I apply the salve gently in the center of the bump, and just like all the times before, Aye-vah winces. At the sight of her pain, I am so enraged that I want to shred that log with my claws for being in the way of her head as she fell. Had she landed on sand, her injuries would be milder.

I dig my claws into my palms, suppressing the growl that threatens to escape my lips. She needs rest.

My precious inara. She has the healing touch, not me. It is not that I mind caring for her. Truthfully, I am glad I have the opportunity to do so; Aye-vah has spent no time prioritizing her own needs—everyone else will always come first. I suppose it is the healers' instinct that lives within her bones, the same instinct I both admire and fear within my mother. But I never want to be the reason that Aye-vah suffers. That is what fills my heart with sorrow. I should be the source of her smiles, her delicate laughter, and her radiating joy. I lift my hand to her face and trace the slope of her small nose with my finger.

"I promise, inara, I shall never let you down again," I vow with a whisper. "You are my world, my light. I will never let harm come your way. For the rest of my days, I shall keep you safe."

I drop my hand and take hers. Her skin is warm, not clammy, which is a good sign. There appears to be no fever or infection to fret over. I trace the strange lines on her palm, smiling at how much I adore this tiny hand and its many fingers. The human females looked so strange to me at first, even Aye-vah. My heart knew she was mine, my body knew that she would feel perfect against me, but my mind still wondered, *why are their faces so very flat? Why is their skin frail like paper?*

I still wonder these things sometimes, but I am less perplexed by them now. The answers to these questions do not matter. Aye-vah is mine, and everything about her is divine.

"Ahlvo?" she asks, her voice dry and her lips chapped as she stares at me with confusion swirling in her eyes. "What... what happened?"

CHAPTER 18

AVA

Ahlvo stares at me in awe, sitting on his hover seat next to the bed, leaning over the edge.

He blinks, not saying anything, and I wonder if I'm still dreaming. This doesn't feel like the dream I was just having though. In the dream, I was at an amusement park with Beyoncé and there was only one soft pretzel left at the pretzel stand, and I took it. I straight-up took it from her. I felt terrible, and she looked at me with sheer disappointment. I didn't think anything could feel worse than that, but now that I'm awake, my head feels like it was hit with a hammer and my arms are so itchy I could rip them out of their sockets. I'm tempted to return to the dream, but the way Ahlvo looks at me…

"You hit your head, Aye-vah," Ahlvo finally replies, "on a log that I will soon destroy. You were bleeding. And now you have a bump, here." He points to it without touching me. I reach up, and not gently enough, glide my fingers over the swollen skin. It throbs so hard that I have to pinch my eyes closed and focus on my breath before opening them again.

When I do, I notice smaller red bumps covering my forearms underneath a thick layer of clear gel. Healing salve, I assume.

Then I remember the bugs.

Those unspeakably hideous bugs with all the feet and the red wings. The feel of those wings stuck to the roof of my mouth returns, and I gag at the memory.

"Aye-vah! Are you well? Do you need to use the waste box?" Ahlvo questions nervously.

I hold up a finger, requesting a moment while I combat the wave of nausea.

"Okay, I'm good now," I tell him. "Why didn't you tell me there were nasty-ass bugs by the lake?"

Ahlvo's lip quirks up on one side, amused. "Are you referring to these bites?" he asks, gesturing to my arm.

"Um, yeah!" I croak. "If I had known there were centipedes with wings and teeth on this side of Oluura, I would've stayed the fuck inside."

"They are called riahpu flies. I do not know why they bit you," he says. "They have always been harmless to us while we are here. They fly around us, but never land."

"Well, where I come from, harmless to one does not mean harmless to all," I tell him. Then my memories click into place. "Oh, well... I may have uncovered their shell after kicking the sand. Then I kind of cracked it open. I was trying to help, I swear... I was going to move the shell into a hole I dug up, but that fell apart, and they swarmed me."

Ahlvo chuckles, and then quickly tries to cover it with a serious expression. He fails and smiles widely. "Well, if you had not crushed their home, I do not think they would have bothered you."

I hate that he's probably right. Clearly my attempt to "save" those damn flies seemed to them like a giant home intruder breaking down the door. If I were those bugs, I would've feasted on my flesh too, I suppose.

Still, I think I'll pass on lake house visits for the foreseeable future once we get back home.

Home.

The word doesn't even make me think of Earth anymore. I'm not sure when that happened, but on some level, I think I knew right away that I wanted to stay on Oluura.

Ahlvo puts the healing salve away, grabs the mug next to the bed, and holds it to my lips. "Drink," he commands, slipping his big hand behind my neck and guiding me into a slightly raised position.

I gulp the water down, and Ahlvo tells me to drink slower. I don't want to—I'm so thirsty, I feel like I could drink a swimming pool. I empty the mug, and Ahlvo takes it over to the spigot and refills it before returning to my side.

"How long have I been out?" I ask.

"A day," he tells me. Then his face falls. "I am so sorry, Aye-vah. I am the cause of your pain."

Huh?

From what I recall, I was the one who confessed my love for Ahlvo, promptly freaked out, kept talking so he couldn't reject me, and then bolted from the house, running straight into a bug's nest.

"How is this your fault?"

"I let you walk away from me without telling you the truth."

I sigh and brace for heartbreak.

His eyes don't hold sympathy or pity, though, like I expected. They're warm, and I focus on the mesmerizing flecks of gold in his violet irises. "You are my inara. I have known from the very first time I laid eyes on you. And I want you, all of you, for the rest of my days."

What? My breath catches in my throat, and I remain frozen.

He takes my hand and rubs small circles into my palm with his thumb. "You are more than I ever could have imagined. I did not think I would find my mate, or that she existed at all. But my wildest dreams could not have created anyone like you."

Me? I'm his inara? The question punctuates every proceeding thought. I can't believe Ahlvo and I have loved each other since the beginning. I want to say so many things in this moment.

Finally, I ask, "You knew since the first time you saw me? Why didn't you say something?" My tone is accusatory, which is not my intention, but admittedly, I am a little pissed that he waited. This entire time we could've been together, and it might've helped with his recovery to have me inside his mind. Yet we've each been miserable—together but still apart.

"Because of that first night on the ship," he says, pulling back his hands and placing them on his thighs. "Do you not remember? You said you appreciated finally having friends by your side who you could trust. I wanted to be that for you." He adds almost too quiet for me to hear, "I also did not feel worthy of being your mate."

"What?" I ask, shocked that the ever-charming playboy would deem himself unworthy of me. "Why? What would make you think that?"

He wrings his hands, not looking at me, and says, "I am not the male I once was. Not the warrior I used to be. I cannot protect you from this hover seat. I have been a terrible patient and do not know why you tolerate my rudeness."

"Ahlvo," I say, taking one of his hands in mine. "You are more than what your body can do on the battlefield. You have been stubborn because you're dealing with the trauma of your leg being blown up by an evil king. I don't hold that against you."

He nods, but still doesn't seem convinced.

"I don't need you to protect me. That's not why I fell for you," I tell him. "You make me laugh. You put me at ease. We come from different backgrounds and different planets, but there are things we understand, things we have in common that others don't." Then I add, "And you're also very pretty."

He dips his chin and a blush appears on his golden cheeks. "I did not wish to scare you by confessing how much you meant to me when you had been so recently betrayed by your Earth mate."

"Not my mate," I clarify. Thinking about my ex, it seems insane that we were ever planning a life together. Compared to how I feel about Ahlvo, I didn't love Ben at all. Like, not even a little. I was excited for our wedding, not because he was the one waiting at the end of the aisle, but because I wanted the wedding. I wanted an entire day where I could twirl around in a pretty dress and feel like a queen. I wanted to be wanted. And as long as I said and did the right things, he wanted me. "He was just," I pause, trying to find the right words, "a nice-enough guy who asked me to marry him at a time when I thought I should already be married. He felt safe. And then he cheated on me."

Ahlvo moves closer. His pouty, soft lips only about an inch from mine. "And how do I feel?" he asks with a heated gaze.

I think about how my heart thumps wildly inside my chest each time he looks at me. I think about how comfortable I feel when we tease each other or when he calls me "noodle." Or the way my body fits against his muscled frame while we sleep. I think about how, if the universe were to implode tomorrow, there's no one else I'd want by my side.

I swallow my fear of being vulnerable. This is the time for honesty. This is when I should tell him I don't want kids. He deserves to know before we get too far into this whole mate thing. My lips part, and I will the words to slip through them, but Ahlvo is looking at me like I'm the only thing that matters, and I don't want to see his face fall when I tell him the truth. I'm normal to him right now. I don't want that to change. So instead, I offer a different truth. "You feel like *everything*."

His eyes meet mine seconds before he leans down to cover my lips with his. The kiss is achingly tender. Our tongues meet, and I gasp into his mouth the moment I feel his fang brush against my bottom lip. Then his lips are everywhere, moving down my jaw and neck, and then back up where he peppers my face with light kisses. I want so much more. I want all of him, so I take control and start kissing his neck as I tug on the bottom hem of his shirt.

He grabs my hands and holds them together as he presses his ridged forehead against mine, careful to avoid my bump. "Not yet, inara. I will not fuck you this day."

I let out a frustrated whimper and he laughs, the sound throaty and low.

"Your fragile human head needs more time to heal," he says, stroking my hair.

I pout like a petulant child, but he's right. I'm fairly certain I have a concussion. But I also want to straddle Ahlvo and lick every inch of his naked chest. "You're gonna confess your eternal love for me and then tell me we can't have sex? Boooo."

"What a stubborn patient you are," Ahlvo says with a smirk.

"Yeah, yeah, yeah," I mutter while rolling my eyes.

He leans his forearms on either side of me, caging me in. "Aye-vah," he murmurs into my ear, "I have waited what feels like a lifetime to see all of your lovely skin, to taste your sweetness on my tongue, and to be so deep inside your cunt that your voice grows hoarse from screaming my name."

I moan at his words.

Ahlvo steals a quick kiss, and says, "The moment you are fully healed, you will be mine."

I suck in a breath, my pussy gushing at his promise of what's to come.

He guides his hover seat to his side of the bed and pulls the covers back. As he climbs in, I notice how swollen his knee looks. "What happened? Did you fall on it?"

Panic rises in my chest as I picture Ahlvo walking, or running, or practicing with his sword, or something else foolish while I was unconscious. I'm out of commission for one day—

"When I heard you scream, I flew my hover seat toward you," he interrupts my accusing thoughts. "But I may have neglected to open the door first."

My eyes go to the front door of the cabin, and while it's mostly intact, the hinge on the bottom of the door frame hangs loose. I don't know if I should laugh.

"I am still in the process of repairing it," he says as his eyes hold mine. "I needed to get to you. I found you lying in the sand, and I picked you up and flew back here. I did not even think about it."

Guilt strikes me in the chest. He hurt himself trying to save me. "Let me take a look. We should probably change your bandages. And did you take your med—"

He puts up his hands, trying to get my attention. "Aye-vah, Aye-vah. Please. I am fine. It is a bit of swelling. That is all."

I drop my hands and sigh because it could've been so much worse. "Okay, but I still want to take a closer look at it in the morning."

He nods, looking slightly amused, and pulls me into his arms once he's under the covers. "It seems we are both difficult patients," Ahlvo whispers as he kisses my hair. "You must let me care for you, my pretty mate."

I press my head onto his chest and inhale deeply. Ahlvo's scent is like a drug. It's spicy and fresh, like a mixture of cayenne pepper and pine trees. I will never tire of it. "Mmm," I murmur with my eyes closed as I lace my fingers through his. This is where I get to fall asleep every night for the rest of my life? Lucky me.

"Aye-vah?"

"Hmm?"

"Who is Bee-yawn-say? You spoke the name in your dreams."

My eyes snap open. "I did?" I ask, surprised that my pretzel dream turned me into a sleep talker.

"Is this a deity humans pray to on your planet?" Ahlvo asks in a hopeful tone.

I smile against his chest. I'm too sleepy to launch into all the wonders of Beyoncé, and too eager to wake tomorrow and finally worship his body, so I say, "Yes."

CHAPTER 19

AHLVO

"**A**nd that's the chicken dance. Humans tend to do that one at weddings," Aye-vah says, resting her hands on her knees with heavy breaths.

"What is a weh-ding?"

"A human mating ceremony, essentially," she replies as she wipes beads of sweat from her brow.

The moment she awoke this morning, she sprung from the bed, moved the chairs away from the fire pit and began shaking out her limbs, testing the strength of her body. This is the fourth "popular human dance" she has shown me since, as proof that she is healed enough from her head injury to mate.

"That one is my favorite, I think," I tell her.

These dances are quite strange, but I have been enjoying the way Aye-vah's body jiggles and sways while she dances. Her breasts, her rounded belly, her bottom, and her legs—my mate's curves are generous and magnificent.

It is not just her beauty that dazzles me in this moment, however. Her shoulders are loose, her smiles come easily, and her spirit feels lighter, less burdened. This is my Aye-vah completely whole, I realize. And her wholeness steals my breath.

I extend my hand to her, and she takes it. I pull her toward me, and she sits sideways across my thighs, turned to face me. Wrapping one arm around her waist and cupping her cheek with my other hand, I lean in and whisper, "Consider yourself healed, pretty noodle."

She lets out a breathy groan before her lips crash onto mine. She is eager, my mate, and my cock surges in response. I fist her tight curls as I swipe my tongue at her closed lips. She pulls back suddenly. "Am I too heavy for your lap? How's your leg? Is it okay?" she asks, frantically glancing down between us.

"Aye-vah," I say as I crook my finger under her chin, bringing her gaze up to meet mine. "I could lift you with one hand and hold you in my palm like a tiny bird. You feel perfect here. And my leg is fine. If it hurts, I shall tell you."

"Oh, okay," she moans dreamily before attacking me with her mouth again.

Her kisses are demanding, passionate, as if she is trying to swallow me. And I want her to. Our tongues clash and tangle, and her grip around my neck tightens as she writhes against me. I pull her closer, and then growl when I cannot press her cunt against my cock. Her leg is in the way.

Righting this wrong, I lift her easily above my lap. As she hangs in the air, she lets out a gasp, but then her eyes brighten and her pupils dilate. My mate likes being lifted. I make a mental note of that.

I settle her on my lap so she straddles me and our mouths find each other again, frenzied at the broken connection. I palm her breast, massaging it as she mewls softly into my mouth. I roll her hardened nipple between my fingers through her tunic, and her blunted claws dig into my scalp. She pulls back just enough to tug her tunic over her head and toss it to the floor before she is on me again, tracing my pointed ear with her tongue. Her breath is hot on my neck, and I shudder, my hips jerking in response.

"Aye-vah," I groan as my fangs extend. I am so desperate to sink them into the smooth skin of her neck that I feel I will die if I do not. "Your taste… I shall never get enough."

She gently pushes my head down so I am eye level with her

breasts, and I lick my lips as I gaze upon her dark brown nipples. They are slightly darker than her rich brown skin and equally mesmerizing. "Stunning," I whisper against her chest before taking her nipple into my mouth and sucking, hard. She cries out as I work the other nipple with my hand. Her breasts are small, but firm, and I love how they fit inside my hand.

"Fuck, Ahlvo!" she shouts, her eyes pinched shut in ecstasy. "Your tongue."

I move to her right nipple giving it equal attention, and Aye-vah begins to writhe harder against me, the friction of our clothing causing my sac to tighten and precome to soak my pants.

Her hands go to the hem of my tunic, and I lift my arms so she can pull it off. Once my chest is bare, she leans back in my lap, and while her eyes take me in, she nibbles on her bottom lip.

She chuckles and says, "Sometimes I can't believe you're real."

I place her hands on my chest, one at a time. "I am real. And I am yours. Do with me as you please."

She traces my abdominal muscles with a finger and murmurs, "Mmm, yum."

I pull her close, pressing our naked chests together, reveling in the feel of her hardened nipples against my skin. I inhale her scent and lick at her neck, envisioning the place where I'll mark her as mine forever.

Aye-vah shimmies out of my lap and ends up kneeling before me. She traces her lips with her tongue and reaches for the waistband of my pants. I know what she is about to do. Varrek told me about Cloh-ee putting her mouth on his cock and how incredible it felt. "No," I say, placing my hand over Aye-vah's to stop her.

"No?" she repeats, hurt flashing in her eyes.

"I will not come before you do. That will not happen." There has been a constant jolt of arousal shooting through my cock since Aye-vah first sat on my lap, but her needs matter, and they will always come first. "Get on the bed," I command.

She leaps to her feet, rips off her leggings, and hops on the bed, her smile wide and bright. My mate also likes being told what to do. Interesting.

I guide my hover seat to the side of the bed and maneuver myself down next to Aye-vah atop the furs. Scooting down a bit, I get my body into position. Aye-vah looks at me, expectantly. "Where do you want me?" she asks, her eyes hooded with lust.

A steady growl emanates from my throat at the sight. "On my face," I tell her.

That surprises her. She seems taken aback and blinks at me. "You mean…"

"You will sit on my face," I instruct. "I will lick your cunt until you come."

She groans at my words, and slowly, hesitantly, swings her leg over me and climbs up my body until her cunt hovers above my mouth. I marvel at the sight, the dark curls at the apex of her thighs are fascinating. Our females do not have this, and even though I have been with females from many planets, this is entirely new to me. I like it, though. Her scent is strongest here within these soft curls.

Aye-vah braces her hands against the wall in front of her and rests her knees next to my ears. I pet her lower mane once, twice, enjoying the downy feel of it before spreading her glistening lips. She quivers. The sight of her wetness causes my cock to thicken and harden, the need to be inside her practically consuming me. I find her bud at the top of her cunt, or her "clit" as the humans call it, and stroke my thumb over it. Her hips buck in response, and I groan, imagining all the ways I plan to play with this clit. What a magical bundle of nerves.

I lick inside her, from the bottom of her seam to the top, and flick my tongue rapidly against the hood of her clit.

"Ahh *yes*!" Aye-vah cries out, her body writhing, already moving faster against my mouth. I look up at her face scrunched in pleasure, her head thrashing in the air, and her eyes closed.

I alternate between flicking my tongue against her clit and lapping at her center, desperate to taste every drop of her sweetness. Aye-vah tastes warm, rich, and slightly tangy, like a piece of fresh fruit under the bright sun. She rides my tongue harder, and I drink her down, exploring her folds and the depths of her heat.

I push a finger inside her cunt, and it slides in easily, she is so wet.

I add another. They drive in and out as I press my tongue against her clit, flicking and tracing and sucking. She screams my name.

Aye-vah sucks in a breath, and her thighs start to shake as she presses them against either side of my head. I suck on her clit harder now, fucking her with my fingers in a steady rhythm. I watch in awe at how her breasts bounce as she rides my face, how her hands curl against the wall. She drenches my fingers, and her body makes wet sounds as I move in and out of her. She is close, and I want to give this to her.

I brush my fang against the hood of her clit and she comes for me. Her nectar floods my tongue and covers my nose and cheeks. I could survive on her juices alone… I am certain they would sustain me. She bangs her hands against the wall, and her head continues to thrash as she rides out her orgasm, and all the while, I keep licking, making it last. The walls of her cunt clench around my tongue, demanding it remain inside her, and I am happy to oblige.

After several moments, her body stills, and she slowly climbs off my face so she can move down to rest her head on my chest. I wrap my arms around her limp body and stroke my hand up and down her back as her breathing returns to normal.

"That was fucking incredible," Aye-vah mutters against my chest, her tone sleepy and content. It seems for a moment that she has fallen asleep, but then she sits up and rolls her hips, her wetness dripping down my stomach. "Your turn," she says with a seductive grin.

"Here," I say, lifting her off me and laying her on her side in front of me. I copy her position, my chest to her back, and move closer until my cock is nestled between the cleft of her ass.

She spreads wide for me, carefully draping her right leg over my injured leg. "Is your leg okay like this?"

"Yes, my mate."

I hold my hand against her belly and slide it down until I feel her wet curls between my fingers. She wraps her arm around my neck and pulls my lips toward hers. It is a brief kiss, but tender. It reminds me of the mating mark I long to give her, and my mouth moves lower, kissing and licking until I reach the spot between her neck and shoulder. This is where I shall mark my mate. But not this day. Our mating ceremony will come later.

I take my cock in hand and slowly guide it through her wet folds, seeking the entrance to her core. I glide it up to her clit, and back down to the end of her seam, coating it with her wetness. She is soaked, and I have no doubt she will be able to take all of me.

I slip inside her carefully, so as not to hurt her. Her cunt is so tight, her heat so intense, I almost come right then, and I am not even all the way in. Aye-vah groans, arching her back, pushing herself farther onto my cock.

I growl into the back of her neck as I pull out slightly, hold for a moment, and thrust all the way in. Her inner walls clench around my cock as if desperate to keep me in place, possessing me as hers.

I feel myself begin to vibrate inside her cunt, and she lets out a long, deep moan. "Oh… oh god. I didn't… I didn't know…" she babbles as she slams her hips back against my thrusts, meeting me with matching intensity.

She feels too good, I cannot last much longer.

Again, her body starts to quiver, and her movements become erratic, and I know she is close to another orgasm. I shall not hold back any longer, I decide. Normally, I would try to give her at least two more orgasms before coming myself, but her cunt is too perfect, her body too welcoming. I don't want to hold back when we could share this.

I slam into her over and over. The slap of her ass against my thighs fills the room, and just as she appears to go over the edge, I press a thumb into her clit, pushing her over completely.

She lets out a scream, her walls squeezing my cock like she never wants to let me go, and my sac tightens in response.

I pull out of her just in time, and my seed juts out in silver streams all over her thighs, and down to her thick calves. I moan at the sight of my spill as I pump into my hand. Her body still shakes against me, but she reaches between us to replace my hand with hers. She strokes me up and down, wringing the last of my come from my body.

Then she turns in my arms, nuzzling her head on my sweat-covered chest as our breaths slowly transform from short pants to long, relaxed breaths. I pull her body higher, bringing our eyes level, and lean in to rub my nose up along the side of her neck and into her hair. I lower until I reach my favorite spot, my marking spot, between her neck and shoulder.

I nibble there, and I feel Aye-vah tense.

"Ahlvo?" she asks, and my heart quickens with fear. Does she not want to complete the mating bond after all?

She turns slightly, so her eyes can meet mine. "I don't want to make this official just yet. I want to complete the bond, I do, but I…" she trails off.

"You what?" I ask nervously. "Tell me."

"I want a wedding first," Aye-vah says in a rush.

"The human mating ceremony you spoke of before?"

"Yeah, it's essentially a party, but with a ceremony where we make promises to each other. How we'll love each other forever. And we dress up all fancy. And there are dances, like those I showed you." She smiles as she describes this custom, and I begin contemplating ways to give this to her. "I was thinking we could complete the mating bond after the wedding?" she asks, her eyes pleading. "We can still have sex in the meantime without completing the bond, right?"

"Yes. We will just not exchange bites until we have our wedding," I tell her. "Do you wish to have the wedding here or in the village?"

"Oh, in the village. Definitely," she says, her tone certain. "We need the clan there. I need the girls by my side. They're my family. And maybe Varrek and Chloe can make a toast or can give us away. Ooh, and we need some Latin in our vows, for sure."

Aye-vah continues listing elements of her ideal wedding, most of which I do not understand, but that one in particular piques my interest. "Lah-tin? This is a language?"

"Yes!" she squeals with glee. "Technically it's a dead language, so not many people use it, but I learned it in school and I love it."

"Why did you learn it if it is not used?" I ask, puzzled.

She rolls her eyes, playfully, and explains. "It's an old language, and every word is fun to say. Plus, it was an extra thing that helped me get into college."

I can imagine my Aye-vah falling in love with a language. Her mind is constantly hungry for new things to learn, and she approaches each challenge with impressive optimism. A magnificent creature she is. "What is your favorite Lah-tin word?"

"It's a phrase, actually. *In perpetuum et unum diem,* and it means, 'forever and a day,'" she says wistfully. "I always thought it would be romantic to include it in my wedding vows, you know?"

"Then we shall include this Lah-tin phrase," I promise her. "And our wedding will be everything you have imagined."

CHAPTER 20

AVA

I have a mate. And we're getting married! It's impossible to hide my smile as the realization hits me for the hundredth time since we discussed it yesterday. When I told Ahlvo that it was important to me to have a wedding before we complete the mating bond, I meant it. I really do want a wedding. I've dreamed of having one since I was a kid. Completing the mating bond here, away from everyone we love, and then coming home like we eloped would feel strange to me. Like the beginning of our life together was done out of order. I want to start the way that feels right.

But it's not the only reason I suggested delaying the mating bond. I need to tell Ahlvo that I don't want kids, and this buys me a bit more time. And I will tell him. I just need to find the right words. Hopefully they'll come to me soon.

I look at Ahlvo, my future alien husband, and sigh, imagining I'm a lovesick cartoon with my hearts popping out of my eyes.

Soon. I will tell him soon.

He's sitting in his hover seat in the corner of the cabin, laser-focused on the comm line repairs since we still haven't been able to connect to the village or Trovilia. We had to add a few extra coats of paste to the wire cover this morning, but Ahlvo is optimistic that it's almost ready to go.

Without looking up from his work, he says, "I can smell your arousal, inara. Do you need me?"

I put my mug of tea down and stroll over to him. "I'll always need you," I purr as I straddle him on his hover seat, my hands on his bare chest. My hands are on him constantly, stroking, petting, massaging. I can't seem to stop touching him, and nor do I want to.

He tosses his tools aside and wraps his big arms around me as he nuzzles my neck. He told me this morning that this is his third favorite part of my body, because my natural scent is strongest here, following closely behind my ass and my thighs. I have no idea what my natural scent is, but I'm glad he likes it. When he said my thighs were his second favorite, I was shocked.

I've never been embarrassed of my cellulite-covered thighs, necessarily, but I've never embraced them either. Ahlvo says he loves the way they shake when I walk, the feel of them squeezing his head while I'm sitting on his face. His hands are on them now, gripping and massaging and staring at them with an appreciative gaze.

And while his eyes are on my legs, I turn slightly so I can peek at his. Ahlvo's leg is almost completely healed. There's still a bit of swelling from when he plowed through the door, but the wound has closed, the scabs are starting to fall off, and what remains is just a large, jagged scar above his knee in a range of gold shades and some slight bruising.

We started on basic physical therapy techniques and stretches after breakfast, but since I don't have much experience in that area of medicine, I urged Ahlvo to take it slow, which is the hardest part of this whole experience, frankly.

He is convinced that because his wound is no longer open, he's fine to move around at his own pace. But even a short walk around this one-room cabin tires him out.

Because of this, we haven't decided when to leave. He's eager to get back to the village so we can begin planning the wedding, and ultimately solidify our mating bond, but I know once we return, so will his depression and anxiety triggers. He'll be close to the training grounds again. He'll be near Varrek and forced to watch Bruvix filling in as second-in-command.

I don't want him to regress. He's in such good shape out here, mentally and emotionally, and I want to enjoy it while it lasts. It's not that I'm tempted to bail once things get difficult. He's my mate, and when I vow to be by his side in sickness and in health, I'll mean it. I just want to linger in this romantic bubble where all we do is eat, sleep, do chores, and have sex.

Ahlvo interrupts my mental montage of the sex we had through the night, and then again this morning, by lifting the bottom of the tunic I'm wearing as a dress and stroking his thumb against my clit. I grip his broad shoulders, pressing my lips to his. His tongue immediately enters my mouth and wraps around mine, stroking and twisting. His hand goes into my hair and he gives it a light tug, just how I like, and I suck in a breath. My clit throbs against his palm as he inserts a finger into my core, and then a second.

"Mmm, you are ready for me, Aye-vah," Ahlvo says against my lips with a cocky chuckle.

"Always, lion man," I reply.

He growls for me, low and menacing, as his heated gaze pins me in place. A chill rolls up my spine and goose bumps cover my flesh. He tugs my tunic over my head and then his mouth is hot on my breasts. He licks and sucks until my nipples form aching points beneath his tongue. My body moves on its own, pressing against him, while I lift and lower onto his fingers. His pants are still on, but he's hard as steel beneath the fabric and I want him inside me. Now.

I reach down and loosen the ties at his waist as his tongue licks at my earlobe. "You want my cock, inara? You want me to fill that tight, hot cunt of yours?" His voice is a husky rumble, and his dirty talk makes me gasp.

"Yes, Ahlvo. Please," I beg as I pull his pants down enough to free him. I bite my lip as his dick springs forward, still not quite used to the sight of him. The first time we had sex, I almost passed out at how big he is. I have no idea how something the size of my arm is able to fit inside me without killing me, but it did, and I survived.

I reach down and take him in hand, stroking slowly down to the base. He's a darker gold here and hairless. He's also slightly curved, which hits me in all the right spots, especially with all that vibrating. My mouth waters at the sight of his sparkly silver precome.

"Tell me, Aye-vah," he commands darkly. "Say it."

I kiss him, hard and quick and then whimper, "I want you inside me. Fill me up, Ahlvo, please."

I lift my body and guide his cock to my entrance. Then in one motion, I sink all the way down. "Oh god. So good," I pant as Ahlvo grips my ass possessively in his hands and hisses through gritted teeth. I start to move up and down, impaling myself on his hard length and releasing a series on unintelligible sounds. Some are gasps, the rest—I don't know, don't care. All I can focus on is how good he feels, stretching me from the inside.

"Aye-vah, my Aye-vah, you hold heaven within your body," he whispers against my breast as he bites down softly on my nipple. The sensation sends a jolt straight to my clit, and I cry out, not caring how loud I am. Another reason not to return to the village. Then I'm riding him hard as he vibrates inside me. The pace is fast and feral as I chase my release. Ahlvo presses a finger against my clit and traces a circle around it, applying pressure the entire time before swiping it from left to right.

I scream as I tumble off the edge. Stars dance behind my eyelids as I dig my nails into Ahlvo's back and ride out the rest of my orgasm.

I feel him take over beneath me as I start to come down, his thrusts becoming harder and faster as he grips my back and breathes heavily into the crook of my neck.

Ahlvo lets out an untamed roar as he lifts me and pulls out. The moment our bodies are disconnected, I lean forward and push my breasts together as his come spurts all over them. I rub his hot silvery seed into my skin until my chest is completely covered and sparkly.

We still don't know if humans and Trovilians are compatible for procreation, but if there's a chance we are, I don't want us to have any surprises.

He pulls me down until our chests are pressed together and his arms are wrapped around me. His heavy breathing matches mine, and we hold onto each other for dear life as we resurface to reality. A light sweat coats our bodies, and normally this would make me self-conscious, but with Ahlvo, I don't give it a second thought. It's another indication of how thoroughly and efficiently we cherished each other's bodies.

Hours after we've bathed together and had lunch, Ahlvo is back at it with the comm line.

I'm hearing a lot of *hmm* and *ah-ha*! over in his corner, but each time I offer to help, he declines, saying he's almost got it. I let him tinker as I organize our dwindling food stash and gather the empty mugs of tea and water that have accumulated around the bed.

A sudden clap sounds from behind me and I turn to see Ahlvo staring at the comm line with a triumphant look in his eyes.

"Did you get it to work?" I ask.

"I did. I did indeed."

I rush over and plop onto his lap as he fires up the screen pad. The message icon lights up with several new messages, and I hold my breath as Ahlvo presses play.

The first one is from Chloe. She's sitting in Varrek's bedroom and her hair is mussed, her eyes bright. "Heyyy, girl! I know we're supposed to leave you alone while you and Ahlvo are at the lake house but I miss you like crazy! Hope Ahlvo isn't giving you too much trouble. Get some sleep. Love you, byeee."

Ahlvo and I laugh as the second message begins. It's also from Chloe. Her skin is slightly pallid and dark circles lurk beneath her eyes. "Ava! Hi, hi, hi. Sorry to bug you again, but I've been tired and a little woozy lately, and Varrek is freaking out. He won't listen when I tell him it's just because we're in the wet season and rain makes me sleepy. He wants me to see Kaiva, and I probably will, but I was hoping if you had a free sec that you could tell him it's no big deal. Just a human thing. And to maybe calm the fuck down. Okay, anyway, love you, bye!"

Ahlvo snickers beside me. "Varrek must be a mess of nerves," he says.

The third message plays. Chloe again: "Hello, my gorgeous cupcake!" she says with a mouthful of junasii bread. She's sitting in the food hall, and it's raining. "OMG, I would kill a bitch for a cupcake right now. I'm bored. Hope you and Ahlvo are having fun at the lake. Love you."

The next one is from Kaiva. "My son, I cannot express how angry with you I shall be if you do not listen to Aye-vah's instructions. I know you can be stubborn, but she is there to help you." Her eyes soften at the last part. "She cares for you very deeply. I hope you are able to see past your own frustrations and let her assist in your recovery."

Ahlvo and I wear matching smiles after hearing Kaiva's voice, and her stern but loving warning that he better do as I say. "Good thing you listened to me," I tease.

He leans in and kisses my cheek as the next message begins. "Um, hi. It's–it's me again," Chloe says in a tense tone and my stomach drops. "So, I'm pregnant." There's a long pause, and Ahlvo and I exchange a wide-eyed glance. "Yeah, bananas, right?" Then she starts laughing. "I just couldn't wait any longer to tell you. I'm going to be a mom! With an alien baby!" she yells.

"Holy shit," I whisper. Chloe's going to have an alien baby. She's going to be a mom. That means we're compatible with the Trovilians when it comes to procreation. That means mated couples can have kids. And I-I might be expected to have Ahlvo's baby. Their race is dying out here on Oluura, and I'm about to become Ahlvo's mate, so… will I even have a choice in the matter? Will I be forced to have a baby? What if I say no? Will the clan hate me? Will I be banished? My breathing picks up and my palms start to sweat as Chloe keeps babbling excitedly. "Anyway, I can't wait for you to come home. Miss you and love you. Byeee!"

"A human-Trovilian child," Ahlvo says in awe. "What a miracle."

"Mm-hmm, yeah. It's wonderful," I say, trying to sound as enthusiastic as Ahlvo. I really am happy for Chloe and Varrek. I'm just not sure what it means for me.

Ahlvo wraps his arms around me and squeezes. "The village will someday have many little ones running around." He sighs wistfully. "I never imagined I would see that again."

"Can't wait," I say, hoping Ahlvo is too distracted by the picture in his head that he didn't notice my flat tone. I don't want to look at him, but my eyes find his, and I realize he's studying me. His nose scrunches up slightly, and I try to focus on how cute he looks rather than the crushing weight of the truth I have yet to reveal.

I should tell him. I should do it now. He gave me the perfect opening. I pinch my eyes shut, and suck in a breath. "Ahl—"

"This is the last one." Ahlvo interrupts me just before the message starts to play. "Ava," Chloe says, sobbing. She wipes away the tears streaming down her cheeks and holds her head in her hands. "Ava, you need to come home." My first thought is that she miscarried, and my heart shatters at the pain she must be feeling right now. "Oh no," I mutter as my eyes fill with tears.

"It's Kate," Chloe continues. "She-she's gone. We don't know where she is. She was here last night and…" she stops as her voice cracks, "and we can't find her. We've looked all over the village. I hope you get this. We need you," her voice lowers. "I–I don't know what to do. Please come home."

The message cuts off, and we sit there silently. "When did she send this?" I ask, my belly tightening with nerves.

Ahlvo looks at the message detail and replies, "This morning."

We share a knowing glance, and Ahlvo grips my hand. I nod. "Let's go."

CHAPTER 21

AVA

Within moments of hearing Chloe's last message, we were up and packing as quickly as we could. We loaded up the ship with everything we brought to the cabin and rushed to free the caught fish before tossing the empty traps inside.

I have no idea how long we've been in the air, but it feels like forever. I can't focus on the beautiful view of Oluura that I couldn't appreciate from the back, because my mind is consumed with thoughts about Kate.

What happened?

Where is she?

Did she wander into the forest again?

Did she run away intentionally?

Was she attacked by a tr'gory?

Is she bleeding out somewhere in the forest?

Or was it that fucking dragon?

I cycle through these questions but rehearsing all the tragic possibilities is making me queasy, so I try to remember the mindfulness meditations I learned in one of my psych classes.

"Sight: the sky, my hands, Ahlvo's braids, my boots, view of Oluura," I say, listing five things I can see from where I sit across Ahlvo's lap.

"What are you doing?" Ahlvo asks, shooting me a look of concern.

"Feel: the fabric of my pants, a headache, my butt on Ahlvo's legs, Ahlvo's hand on my thigh," I continue. "It's, uh, it's a meditation practice for moments of extreme anxiety. It's about engaging your senses and getting out of your head with counting." My palms start to sweat and I realize I need to save my explanation for later, once the panic has passed. "Hear: the engine of the ship, my heavy breathing, boxes and bags shifting in the back."

"Are you okay?" he asks, his grip on my thigh tightening.

"Yeah, later. Later, later. I'll tell you later," I stammer, trying to tune him out. Where was I? Okay, now two things I can smell. "Smell: the fish in the food box and Ahlvo's skin. And taste…" I trail off, trying to figure out if the fish smells bad enough that I can taste it. I can't, so I grab Ahlvo's big hand and press a kiss to his knuckles. "Taste: Ahlvo's sweet skin."

I let out a deep sigh, still clutching his large, warm hand to my chest.

I don't feel completely free of panic, but there's enough room in my lungs to breathe. That's something.

He lifts his other hand off the control levers and runs his fingers through my hair. It's comforting. "All will be well, inara," he vows. "We shall find her."

Verbalizing the fact that Kate is gone hits me like a freight train, and a choked sob escapes me. I become a mess of tears and snot with my arms wrapped around Ahlvo's neck as I cry into his chest.

He doesn't say anything, and I'm glad because there's not much else to say. Nothing will make me feel better until Kate is safely home. Guilt envelopes me as I replay our last conversation. How worn down she seemed. How tortured and hopeless.

If I had stayed in the village, would Kate still be there? I don't even want to entertain the thought, but it's impossible not to. She needed more support. She needed a stronger inner circle. Chloe and I have been so preoccupied lately, and the clan hasn't exactly welcomed Kate with open arms. Or at least, Kate didn't feel like they had. She felt isolated and mocked, like an outcast. She needed us, and we let her down.

Fear surges through my veins at the unknown that lies ahead of us. I have no idea what will happen once we get back. Will we find Kate? Will she be unharmed? Will Ahlvo undo all of his progress by pushing himself too hard? Will he become depressed again, haunted by the reminders that his body is different now?

These are things I don't have control over, and that fills my chest with agony.

"We are close," Ahlvo says quietly as we glide over the mountains, covered in the blue and green trees native to Oluura.

I spot the dense Ga'Nvi forest in the distance, and I feel my shoulders loosen. At least we're home. There's comfort in that despite the chaos.

Ahlvo lands the ship near the others, and I hop off his lap so I can help him maneuver his hover seat out the door. We load our arms with our belongings, and book it to the tree line. It's dark out, but luckily, it's not raining, and I'm praying to every god I've ever heard of that it stays that way until we get back. Just inside the tall trees, we meet up with Varrek, Chloe, and Bruvix. They must have been notified that our ship was approaching through the new security system Bruvix installed.

I drop everything I'm holding and race toward my pregnant friend. "You're home!" she cheers as I wrap her up in a hug.

When I pull back to look at her, we both start weeping. Through tears, I congratulate her on the pregnancy and hit her with question after question about Kate. She doesn't know much beyond what she said in her message, but the hunters have already been sent out to patrol the surrounding areas.

Varrek, Bruvix, and Ahlvo speak in hushed tones off to the side, and Ahlvo is still in his hover seat. I'm pleasantly surprised by this, because I figured the moment he saw Varrek, he'd want to show off how much his leg has healed by running or something.

Bruvix and Varrek take most of the boxes. Chloe holds my bag of clothes since Varrek won't let her carry anything heavier than that, and I sit on Ahlvo's lap and hold the rest as he glides his hover seat through the trees.

Once we reach the main path of the village, it's a somber reunion with several members of the clan. They're thrilled to see us, but it doesn't feel appropriate to celebrate anything. Kaiva's eyes are wide and watery when she sees us together, and she takes each of our hands in hers, crying silently and nodding. She puts her hands on either side of my head and presses her cheek against mine. "You saved him, sweet child. I can see it."

My lip trembles as I nod at her, not knowing what to say. I didn't realize how much her approval meant to me until this moment. I'm glad I didn't let her down.

We make it to the food hall where we find several of the warriors. Nalba and two of the Hexrins, Tibik and Jobaki, (I think her name is), are huddled together at one of the long wooden tables. Varrek places our bags at our feet as he takes his place at the end of the table. Kaiva, Chloe, and Bruvix stand next to us. I resume my place on Ahlvo's lap.

"Fill us in," Ahlvo says, and I shiver at the authority in his voice. I don't often get to hear this particular tone, clearly reserved for his crew, but I definitely dig it.

Varrek straightens his spine and begins. "We currently have Rumo, Kital, Ehnder, Krahn, Ulkii, and Lahkzo patrolling the areas just beyond the forest. They left this morning, and we have not heard anything yet."

"Why are Viltress and Mikarya not with them?" Ahlvo asks, nodding to the female hunters at the other end of the table.

"Because we believe the draxilio is responsible for Kay-teh's disappearance," Varrek states, rubbing a hand down his face. "We do not know the motives of this draxilio, but if it is targeting females, we will not let it take any others."

"Why do you assume it was the dragon?" I ask. "How can you be certain she didn't run away or was attacked in the woods by a tr'gory?"

"If Kay-teh chose to run away, our hunters would have located her by now," Varrek replies. "Or at least, some sign of her. She is a human in unfamiliar territory, and I do not think she would get far."

"She is far too fragile to survive outside the village on her own," Nalba adds. "No human could."

I clench my jaw, not in the mood for Nalba's cracks about how weak we are, but I say nothing because she's not wrong, at least compared to the Trovilians. I think of the bites on my arms and how I managed to anger a family of otherwise peaceful bugs into chewing me up right outside the cabin. Without the proper survival skills, we'd struggle significantly to make it on our own.

Then Tibik speaks up. "Jobaki was the last to see her. She does not believe Kay-teh chose to leave."

"Wait, what?" I shoot up from Ahlvo's lap, as this is new information to me.

Tibik gestures to Jobaki. She's a thin, young looking female with that signature Hexrin maroon hair, golden eyes, and extremely pointy, pierced ears, and I can't imagine she's older than fourteen or fifteen. She stands and clears her throat.

"Kay-teh was tired the eve she disappeared. I saw her stumbling from the trees, yawning and rubbing her eyes," Jobaki says, her eyes downcast and her voice shaky. She doesn't seem fond of being the center of attention. "When she saw me watching her, she yelled at me to leave her alone and that she wanted to sleep." Jobaki sits, drops her chin to her chest, and fidgets with a loose thread on her shirt.

"She wouldn't have made it outside the forest on her own being that sleep deprived," I conclude.

"And tr'gorys are savage beasts," Bruvix notes. "If she had been attacked by one of them, there would be…" he pauses, appearing shaken, "a mess of blood and bones left behind."

I did not want to picture that. Clearly Bruvix didn't either. But I'm glad he said it because I'm relieved to dismiss it as an option.

"So how do we track a dragon?" Chloe asks, taking my hand in hers and squeezing.

"And how do we kill it when we find it?" I add, now eager for vengeance.

Ahlvo chuckles darkly and kisses my temple. "That is my mate," he whispers.

"At first light, the crew will pair up and venture outside the hunters' normal patrol paths. We will cover the mountainside and the hills. Bruvix will take the zip ship and be our eyes from above," Varrek says, and Bruvix nods in agreement. "We will all carry screen pads. Warriors, you are to report anything you find that carries Kay-teh's scent or is evidence that she has crossed the path you are on. You are not to engage the draxilio should you encounter it. You are to report back and wait for the rest of us to arrive. Understood?"

The warriors tap their chests with their fists, and I assume that signifies their acceptance of the mission. The crowd rises from the table and everyone heads off in different directions. I'm not sure what time it is, but it's definitely well past dinner and the warriors will need rest for the search tomorrow.

Kaiva leans down and gives Ahlvo and me a half-hug before heading home. Eventually, it's just Chloe, Varrek, Bruvix, Ahlvo and me at the table.

"What can I do?" Ahlvo asks Varrek. This is the moment I've been dreading. Of course, Ahlvo wants to help find Kate, and I love him for that, but he's not physically able to trek up a mountain in search of a dragon. Even his hover seat is not capable of crossing the brambles of the forest.

"Well, now that you are back, of course…" Bruvix replies, giving Varrek a questioning glance.

Varrek furrows his brow, thinking, and zeroes in on Ahlvo's leg. "Bruvix has served as my second in your absence, Ahlvo, and I want to be certain that any help you provide will not set you back."

"Ah, there is no need to concern yourself with that, brother," he says as he looks at me, beaming with pride. "I have grown quite comfortable on my hover seat. And Aye-vah will tell you that my wound is almost completely healed, so it will be no trouble for me to join the search."

My heart sinks.

"Right, Aye-vah? You said my leg is almost healed, did you not?" Ahlvo asks, his eyes pleading.

What am I supposed to do? I can pull rank and tell Varrek that Ahlvo is not medically cleared for a vigorous hike through the mountains. Then he'll be forced to stay here and continue recovering—which is what I want—but he may resent me for it. At the very least, I will crush his spirit.

Or if I let him determine his own limitations, he could injure himself, causing another setback or something much worse. A terrible image flashes in my mind of him limping over rocks and through trees with his crutch, moving at a snail's pace while trying to conceal how much pain he's in.

I sigh and get off Ahlvo's lap so I can stand. "The wound on his leg is almost completely healed. This is true," I say to Varrek. Then I turn to Ahlvo. "If you truly feel your body can handle this, I will not stand in your way."

He laughs at first, like he wasn't expecting me to offer anything but enthusiastic support. He stares at me for a long moment before he turns back to Varrek, his confident smile returning. "You see? I am healed enough to go."

You can't save him, I remind myself. *He has to be willing to save himself.*

Varrek looks at Bruvix before turning to me. He tilts his head, a million questions in his emerald eyes, and I offer him a slight shrug of defeat. I've given Ahlvo all the help I can. I can't do anymore.

"Very well," Varrek finally utters. "Meet us here at first light. You and I shall search for Kay-teh together."

That's something at least. Varrek knows how to handle Ahlvo, so if he's going to join the search, I'm glad Varrek will be by his side. It's a small comfort, but I'll have to cling to it while Ahlvo traverses a mountain with a hover seat that doesn't go higher than my hip and a crutch that he tires of after an hour.

Varrek and Chloe help us drop our bags inside the front door of the house I share with the girls before heading to Varrek's house. I take a moment to appreciate that familiar scent that now means home, and

I'm so thankful to be here I could cry. We take off our boots, and Ahlvo parks his hover seat next to the stairs. He pulls out his crutch and I let him go up first, ready to assist if he needs it.

"We can sleep in Kate's room tonight if you want," I offer when he lets out a labored breath three steps in. Two flights of stairs will be a lot.

"No, it is fine. I can do it," he replies quickly.

I roll my eyes as far back into my head as they'll go, grateful he can't see me because this is ridiculous. He can barely climb a flight of stairs, and he thinks he can make it up a damn mountain?

We make it into my room, and Ahlvo sighs in relief. I sling my bag off my shoulder and pull out my sleep shirt. I change quickly, and when I turn around, I find Ahlvo sitting on the wooden chest of clothes by the door, staring at his feet.

"You need help getting changed for bed?" I ask, increasingly irritable about everything. I'm tired, I'm afraid for Kate, afraid for Ahlvo, and I just want this day to be over.

He pulls his shirt over his head, and then his eyes meet mine, his lips pursed. "You think I cannot see there is something on your mind, Aye-vah? Why do you not just say it?"

"Oh, you wanna do this now? Fine," I say, rubbing a hand down my face. "I'm pissed that you decided to join the search party. It's reckless, and your leg cannot handle what you're about to put it through."

He scoffs. "Then why did you tell Varrek I am healed enough to go?"

"Because! Because I don't want to spend the rest of our lives telling you what you should or shouldn't do!" I say, throwing my hands up. "Why do I have to play that role, Ahlvo?"

"I thought you were enjoying becoming a healer. Is this not part of that?"

"What, hovering over your shoulder every single day, making sure you don't push yourself too hard? No. That is not part of being a healer."

His chin dips, and he stares at his hands in his lap. "I see. So, you do not believe in me."

Seriously? My fists ball at my sides. "You think I don't believe in you? You think that's all that's needed for you to be able to do this?"

"Well, it would be nice to know that my mate sees me as a capable male," he mutters under his breath.

"This has nothing to do with what you're capable of. This is about you needing to prove something to Varrek, or the clan, or to me… I don't even know." I'm shouting by the end. "This is about your ego, Ahlvo. You're willing to risk your health, and possibly even your life, just so… what? So Varrek doesn't keep Bruvix as his second for this one mission? So he knows you can still protect the clan?"

"He needs me in fighting form. A draxilio taunts our clan. It has taken Kay-teh, your Kay-teh, and all I want to do is help bring her back!" He's shouting now too.

My shoulders slump, exhaustion taking hold. I approach him slowly and crouch before him. "I don't want to fight with you. I really don't. I just think you're prioritizing the wrong things."

He takes my hands in his and brings them to his mouth, placing a kiss on each of my palms. "I know that you will miss me, Aye-vah, but I will not be gone long. I swear it. And then we celebrate our mating properly."

I sigh, dropping my head. "Okay," I start. "I need you to listen carefully. This is not about me missing you. It's not about me not believing you can do this. It's not even about me wanting you to stay off your feet until you're fully recovered."

"Then I do not understand…" Ahlvo trails off.

"I want *you* to choose to stay off your feet until you're fully recovered. I want you to want to take care of yourself. I want you to respect the limitations of your body and meet it where it's at instead of forcing it."

"You think I have not accepted my limitations? How long have I been using this crutch?" He waves his crutch in front of me.

I rub my forehead. "I said 'respect your limitations.' Accepting them and respecting them are not the same. Accepting your limitations is a period at the end of a sentence, a closed door on what you thought you could do or accomplish. Respecting your limitations is a door that's still open. There's space to accomplish your goals at another time, or in a different way, or not at all because your goals have changed entirely. The difference is about defeat versus resolve," I tell him as I trace the small scars on his calloused hands.

He nods but stays quiet.

"I'm not saying you can't help Varrek or your crew. I just... don't want you to help in a way that could cause you more pain. I need you around for a long time, buddy."

He squeezes my hands, and I know there's nothing else I can say. He knows how I feel now, and I hope he really thinks this through. "Come on," I say, pulling him up to stand. "Let's get some sleep."

We crawl onto the bed and under the covers. We both lie on our backs, staring at the ceiling as silence fills the space between my body and his. I close my eyes, dreading the coming day. Just as I'm about to drift off, he reaches for my hand, threading his fingers through mine.

I send a prayer toward the sky, begging that this hand returns to me with this wonderful male attached, in one piece.

CHAPTER 22

AHLVO

Dawn peeks through the leaves of the trees, indicating the time has come to meet Varrek and the rest of the crew. I use my crutch to pull myself to my feet, and I lean on it to tug my tunic over my head.

Aye-vah still sleeps, curled into a ball on her side. Her lips are parted, her small hands tucked beneath her chin. I give her a light shake, and she groans as her eyes blink open.

"Mmm, what time is it?" she asks in her husky morning voice.

I smile as I mesmerize her face, the soft curve of her cheek, the narrow slope of her nose, and the crinkles by her eyes. It is a perfect face; one I will forever treasure seeing the moment I wake. "Time to go," I tell her.

She sits up in a rush, looking around the room as she climbs to her feet. "Okay, yeah, let me just put my pants on, and I'll see you off."

We finish dressing, put our boots on, and I glide my hover seat outside onto the main path. I offered Aye-vah my lap, but she has chosen to walk beside me. The village is quiet with only the sound of my crew's boots trudging through the moss toward the meal hall.

Several crew members are huddled together talking quietly when we arrive. Varrek is about to announce the pairs for the search, but when he sees me, he breaks off from the group and makes his way over to us.

"So, you are ready?" he asks, though he seems to be addressing both me and Aye-vah.

Aye-vah nods at my side, forcing her lips into a smile.

"Actually," I begin, "I shall remain here with the females and the rest of the clan. There should be a warrior here in case Kay-teh returns, if that is acceptable to you."

Aye-vah's eyes go wide at my words. "Wait. What?"

Varrek smiles proudly at me and gives my shoulder a single pat. "Very well, brother. This is a brilliant plan." He trots off toward Bruvix, and my eyes follow. I assume they will pair up instead, and as I watch, I realize there is no envy in my heart.

When I turn toward my mate, I find her gazing at me with all the love and adoration it is possible to communicate with just eyes.

"You are pleased, it seems," I say with a smirk.

"Is this really what you want?" she asks, her voice shaky, as if she is afraid to hear my answer.

"Yes, Aye-vah. This is what I want."

I did not sleep a wink last night. Aye-vah's words played in my head over and over. She is right. I was not respecting my body by asking to join the search. I am in no condition for that kind of strenuous activity. Perhaps if I could walk on my crutch for longer periods of time or if my hover seat could lift higher off the ground, but neither of those are true, and so I shall help the crew from the village.

Aye-vah plops down onto my lap and nuzzles into my neck. "Oh, thank god. Thank you, Ahlvo. Thankyouthankyouthankyou."

I laugh as she peppers my jaw with kisses. "There is no need to thank me, little noodle. I would do anything for you."

She pulls back to look me in the eye. "But I need you to do this for you."

"I am doing it for me, yes. But I am also doing it for you, for *us*." I tell her as I run a finger along her bottom lip. "I never want to be the cause of your sadness again."

She parts her lips and nips at my claw with her little teeth. "Okay, I'm good with that."

"Ahlvo!" Bruvix hollers as he approaches. "Here are the routes each pair will be taking this day," he says as he hands me a map and with several notes on it. "Varrek wanted you to have this."

"Ah, yes. I shall keep track of paths each pair has checked. Thank you," I reply.

"Certainly," he mumbles before rejoining the group.

"Okay, my mate," I say as she hops off my lap. "You go back to bed. I have a job to do."

* * *

"Not a trace?" I ask Varrek and Drasko as they emerge from the forest behind the meal hall. I glide over to them on my hover seat, eager for something, anything to report back to Aye-vah. The late morning air is heavy with humidity, and I wipe the sweat from my temple in frustration.

"Nothing, I am afraid," Drasko replies through panting breaths. He and Varrek are coated in dirt and have been gone since yesterday morning searching for Kay-teh. I grunt as I update my search log and check the route they just completed on the map.

When we first began this rescue mission three days ago, all of the male hunters and warriors went out at the same time. But after their first full day of searching the neighboring hillsides and mountains, I saw how all returned weary and despondent and knew this would not be sustainable.

So I took logistical control of the mission, updating the map with routes we've covered and coordinating the search teams. I pulled the hunters off the search and returned them to their normal schedule. This way we would not run low on food, and they could still report back to us if they came across any sign of her or the draxilio.

Two pairs of warriors leave each morning, going in opposite directions. They are to alert us if they find something, or return after one full day. We have yet to discover a single trace of Kay-teh.

We have, however, come across some new fruits and herbs, as well as a brown fuzzy creature with white spots that enjoys swimming in the river at the bottom of the hill. Its kind lives about a day's trek from the village and is twice the size of a tr'gory. It does not appear to be aggressive, but their claws are frighteningly long, so the warriors who spotted it kept their distance. Still, it is helpful information. Since one of our clansmates was killed by a tr'gory during our first year, we have not fully explored much beyond our immediate surroundings. It did not feel worth the risk. With Kay-teh gone, things have changed.

Unfortunately, the longer we continue this mission without any results, the more I question how much longer we should go on. I have not mentioned this to Aye-vah, because she has made it clear that we cannot end the search until Kay-teh is found. I understand this. The moment we decide to end the search, we are accepting the possibility that Kay-teh is dead, and Aye-vah refuses to do this. She is convinced that Kay-teh is alive but maybe somewhere far away with the draxilio.

The problem I have with this theory, and her need to continue searching no matter how long it takes, is that Aye-vah does not want to have our wedding or solidify our mating bond until Kay-teh returns home. She says she would feel uncomfortable celebrating our future with the clan without Kay-teh. She sees Kay-teh as her family, and I do not want her to be sad on our wedding day—it is the last thing I want my mate to feel on the day we become one. This wedding is important to her, and I want it to be just as she imagined.

The longer we wait to exchange mating bites, the stronger the tether becomes. By waiting, we are essentially denying the mating bond, which will have long-term physical effects on both of us if we continue to do this. From what my mother has heard about other mates who have denied the bond, we will become agitated and our bodies will weaken. It will not kill us, or at least, she does not think so.

A denied mating bond has never lasted long enough to kill the pair, but with our bodies in a weakened state, we will be more susceptible to disease. Since Aye-vah is human, I do not know if she will experience these symptoms, but I have already noticed them in me. But I will not let my inara down. If waiting is what she wants to do, then wait, I shall.

I rub my eyes and then look closely at my fingers. They shake as I hold my hand up, and I know this is yet another symptom of denying the tether. I wave Varrek and Drasko away as I head to the meal hall. Perhaps food will make me feel better.

Waldric engages me in friendly chatter as he piles my plate with meat and bread. I try to listen to what he says, but my mind is elsewhere. It is with Kay-teh, silently begging her to come home. It is cursing the angry fog that still visits me at night before I drift into a fitful slumber, whispering that Bruvix is a much better second than I have ever been. It is picturing my map, searching for routes we have not explored. And then it goes to my Aye-vah with her large, soft thighs and glowing skin, imagining ways I can make our wedding perfect for her.

I have talked to Cloh-ee about human weddings. Aye-vah does not even wish to discuss the wedding until Kay-teh is found, so I have begun planning on my own. Cloh-ee said that weddings have lots of flowers, drinks, food, and pretty clothing. Bruvix has begun working on a special batch of his ale, and I have found a flower that I know Aye-vah will love. It grows in abundance near the falls, and it reminds me of Aye-vah's spirit. I am still working on the food and pretty clothing.

Once I've finished eating, I head back to my mother's house. Not long after Aye-vah and I returned from the cabin, I moved my things into the house the females share. Cloh-ee now lives with Varrek, and with Kay-teh gone, we have a good amount of space. Plus, my mate wanted the privacy. She did not feel comfortable riding my cock in my bedroom at my mother's house, one floor beneath the room my mother and father share. She said it felt like we were in "hi sk-ool." Whatever that is.

You are not a worthy mate for Aye-vah, the fog whispers. *You are weak, stubborn, and the confident stride you used to have is lost forever.*

I grit my teeth, willing the voice in my head to cease talking.

You are not even second-in-command anymore. That makes you nothing. You are nothing.

I stop my hover seat on the main path and rub my eyes. *Go away,* I silently tell the fog. *Go. Away.*

You cannot even find Kay-teh, and if you do not, Aye-vah will never forgive you.

I pinch my eyes closed and rock back and forth as my eyes fill with wetness. I hate that I cannot turn it off. That it finds me and tortures me whenever it pleases.

She will never forgive you, it repeats.

"Ahlvo. Ahlvo!"

I crack my eyes open to find Aye-vah, standing over me, her hands gripping my wrists.

"What's happening?" she asks, her tone filled with alarm.

I open my mouth to tell her, but the fog stops me.

The moment she finds out you cannot handle your own problems, she will leave you, it sneers. *She'll find another male who is stronger, a male who can walk and fight and control his emotions.*

"Ahlvo, five things you can see. Tell me. Right now," Aye-vah commands, snapping her fingers to hold my attention.

"That I can see?" I ask, confused.

Aye-vah nods. "Yes, that you can see. Remember when I did that on the ship? Just list them off. Five things."

"I-I see your big brown eyes, your lips. I see the lever on my hover seat, the blue moss covering the ground, and the front door of our home," I mutter.

Aye-vah smiles and her eyes light up with pride. "Good. Good. Okay, now four things you can feel. Go."

I am tempted to think on this, but I know that is the opposite of what this exercise is for. "Um, the cold steel of my hover seat, the thick cloth of my tunic, the tightness of one of my braids pulling on my scalp, and the sore muscles in my leg."

Aye-vah gently moves my hands so she can sit on my lap. "Good! Okay keep going. Now, three things you can hear."

I nod, refusing to break my focus on my surroundings. "I hear the squishing of moss beneath the boots of my clan. I hear dishes clanging together at the meal hall. And I hear your breath, deep and steady."

"Two things you can smell," Aye-vah says as she lightly runs her fingers up and down my arm.

"I smell your fear for me, the scent thick in my nose. But there is also the intoxicating scent of your mane, and it is calming."

She chuckles, relief softening her features. I feel the beat of my heart return to normal, and now that I am anchored to Aye-vah and how she affects my senses, I do not hear the fog. "Now taste," she purrs.

I put my hand on the back of her neck and pull her to me, brushing my lips against hers. She wraps her arms around my neck and returns my kiss, moaning into my mouth. Goddess, her taste. It is sweeter than the sweetest b'fiko berry, by far.

"Hey!" Nalba hollers from behind us, making Aye-vah jump in my lap. "Do not ravage your delicate human mate in the middle of the path. You have a home for such things."

"Oh," Aye-vah says with thinly veiled irritation in her tone. "Hi, Nalba. What can we do for you?"

"I come with a gift for Ahlvo," she says plainly. "Here."

She pulls a gleaming silver stick from behind her back and holds it out to me. It has a cushioned handle at the top and intricate designs etched along the side. I notice the protection symbol the Hexrins frequently use in their rituals, the flag from my village on Trovilia, and the words *Boz fra puyhivna n bakko. Boz fra qem wa gonnuf. Boz ryu dunikko gpon la xhi,* which translate to "May you fight with honor. May you emerge victorious. May the goddess grant you more time."

"It is a cane." She grabs it from my hands with a huff and begins pointing out the features. "It will help you with your limp."

When she turns it over, I discover a detailed drawing I do not recognize. "What is this here?"

"Ah, I created an Oluuran crest for our clan." Then she smiles wickedly. "And it also does this…"

Nalba presses a small button on the underside of the cane's handle, and the steel surface flips inside itself, revealing a golden pole. I do not understand why this is significant until Nalba points it to the sky, revealing a luminous pointed tip.

Momentarily, I'm shocked and left utterly speechless. "A sword?"

"A sword," she confirms.

I stare at it, my mouth hanging open as sunlight bounces off the sharp tip.

"You are a warrior, Ahlvo," Nalba says. "Your body is different, but it does not mean you cannot fight. That you cannot protect your clan. We shall just create the tools necessary for you and this new body. All the skills you have learned over your life, you will still be able to use them—just differently."

Aye-vah's hand goes to her chest, covering her heart. She seems equally stunned.

Most of the time, I continue to use my hover seat, but when I do my stretches, I find that I am able to move easier. While I have a limp, reclaiming the power to walk feels like a monumental achievement. I thought that was the best I could hope for: being able to stand on my own. But with a cane that doubles as a sword, I...might be able to do more.

"Nalba, I—"

"O fah. Do not thank me," she interrupts, putting up a hand. "This is my home, and I have no interest in leaving it. Or having it attacked under the darkness of night by a fire-breathing beast. I made this so you can continue fulfilling your duty to the clan. To protect us. That is all."

Aye-vah narrows her eyes at Nalba. "That's all, eh?"

"Yes, little human," Nalba replies in a snarky tone.

Aye-vah purses her lips and nods.

I dip my chin and raise the sword horizontally in both hands. It is heavy, but only slightly heavier than the sword I used to use. The blade is smooth and cold against my skin. Immediately, I picture myself in a fight stance, but with my feet closer together, and putting weight on the opposite foot to protect my leg. With practice, I could do this.

Like all of Nalba's creations, the sword is well crafted, the blade balanced and sharp. "It is my honor to protect my people and my home."

Nalba gives an awkward smile and jogs back toward her shop.

Strange one, she is. But brilliant.

* * *

I spend the bulk of the afternoon polishing my cane sword. It is the loveliest weapon I have ever owned. And that is not just because of the intricate shapes and sacred words engraved on the cane or the rich gold shade of the sword. It is because it was made specifically for me, to help me. To protect my leg, so I can protect my clan. I feel as if I have purpose now—a new reason for living. My mind spins as I fantasize about all the ways I plan to use this sword. And I envision slicing my sword through the middle of the angry fog in my mind, silencing it forever. Before this, I doubted I would ever be physically able to participate in battle or practice on the training grounds with the rest of the crew.

Varrek has not said anything to indicate that I am prohibited from doing these things. I merely assumed that those days were behind me. But I am not so sure anymore. Perhaps if I become comfortable with the new way my leg moves and accept when I have hit my limit, I can fight. I can create a new style of fighting. A way that will have my opponents underestimating me, giving me the advantage. They will look at me and see a male with a bad leg, an obvious weakness. They will see an easy target, and assume they can defeat me. They will not know that this thought will be their last. Not until it's too late, anyway.

Perhaps this is what I was always meant to do.

A smile stretches my lips as I ponder the possibilities.

When Aye-vah hollers at me from downstairs that it is mealtime, I push the button under the handle, turning my sword back into a cane, and make my way down to the first level, one stiff step at a time. Aye-vah stands by the door with a hand on her wide, wondrous hip, and looks me up and down.

"You look hot with a cane," she says with a velvety rasp to her voice.

"I do?" I pause at the bottom step, turning and lifting the cane in various poses.

"Mmm," she groans as she wraps her arms around my middle. "Mama likes."

I furrow my brow at her strange saying, but her gaze is heated, and I catch a whiff of her arousal scent, so I am fine with it. I place a kiss on the tip of her small nose as we head outside into the coolness of the night.

"I'm glad it's not raining today," Aye-vah says.

"I am sure it will tomorrow," I reply. My Aye-vah does not enjoy the wet season, but we are only in the early days, and I hope she will come to appreciate the cozy joys of it.

We step onto the main path and run into Varrek and Cloh-ee on their way to the meal hall as well. "Oh, hey, there," Cloh-ee greets us cheerfully.

For a time, we walk together, but when we hear a crunching sound from the forest, Varrek and I stop in our tracks. We are not expecting any warriors or hunters to return at this time, and the rest of the clan has been told to stay within the village.

The bushes on the edge of the forest shake, and then separate, revealing Kay-teh.

It… it is Kay-teh.

She wears a billowing pale green dress that matches her eyes. The dark circles under her eyes are gone, and color has returned to her spotted cheeks. She looks better. Healthier. And trailing close behind her is a large male with blue shimmering scales covering his body.

He has two wide black horns jutting up and curling back from the sides of his head. His hair is short and black, matching his horns. While he carries no obvious weapons, there could be a dagger hidden beneath his tunic or in his boot. He is heavily muscled, and the scowl on his face has me hating him in an instant.

My instincts take over, and I push Aye-vah behind me. Varrek does the same with Cloh-ee. I quickly transform my cane to a sword and step into my modified fight stance. Varrek pulls out a dagger beside me.

Kay-teh gives us a sheepish look and says, "Heyyy." She waves, then looks in the direction from which they emerged. "So, what'd I miss?"

"Kay-teh, step aside!" I shout, preparing to lunge at the male. Varrek moves slowly to the left, beginning to circle him. We have not trained together in some time, but our instincts run deep.

My skin begins to tingle, and I lean on the balls of my feet, poised for attack. A growl rumbles inside my chest, and I scan the male's upper body, looking for the perfect vulnerable spot for my blade.

"No, no, no. That's not necessary, really," she mutters, holding her arms wide to block our view of her abductor. It is futile, though, because Kay-teh's head does not even reach the male's chest.

"Kate, are you okay? Where have you been? What the fuck is going on?" Aye-vah asks as she peeks her head around my shoulder.

"And what has happened to your arm, Kay-teh?" I ask, pointing the sharpened tip of my sword to her elbow. The moment she looks down, Varrek grabs her other arm and pulls, and my target is no longer blocked by a delicate female.

I push off the ground, leaping toward him, quickly closing the space between us. He holds up his hands in surrender, but my sword is primed, its sharp point aimed right for his heart.

CHAPTER 23

AVA

"I'm not calling you a liar. I'm just saying you can tell us the truth. You know that, right?" I tell Kate as Chloe and I sit with her on the bed she hasn't slept in for days. She came back last night, just strolled right out of the forest with that blue dude behind her, acting like she hasn't been missing. Like we haven't been searching tirelessly for her.

Ahlvo was dangerously close to slicing Kate's kidnapper in half, but he jumped out of the way at the last second, Kate rushing to shield him with her body. Since then, it's been impossible getting information from her. We know practically nothing about this "Niro" person, what happened while she was gone, or why he's here with her now.

After lots of shouting and pointing and me keeping Ahlvo from ripping Niro's arms off with his bare hands, we learned that Niro grabbed Kate in the middle of the night and took her back to his home, which is a network of caves inside the mountain closest to us. According to Kate, it was all a big misunderstanding, and Niro hasn't hurt her.

None of us were satisfied with this—and there's still part of me that wants to punch him in the face for kidnapping my best friend—but that's all Kate would say. Niro said nothing beyond where his caves are located.

I'm pretty sure he's waiting for Kate outside the house at this very moment.

The clan is terrified of him, and Varrek doesn't want him here at all. Apparently, Kate and Niro are here partly because they have "something to take care of" with the Hexrins. What that thing is, Kate won't say. What will happen after that "something" is taken care of, Kate also will not say.

"I *am* telling you the truth. I am fine. Perfectly fine," she replies, shooting me an overly dramatic eye roll.

"Bologna foot?" I ask, hoping she remembers our secret password.

"No! No danger. I swear," she sighs, exasperated. "Jeez."

"Hey! None of that. We thought you were dead," Chloe snaps. "Do you have any idea how scared we were? How little we've slept?"

Kate jerks back, surprised at Chloe's stony expression, and turns to me for support. "Nope. I'm with her on this," I say, gesturing to Chloe. "If you were fine, you should've called. Or sent a smoke signal. Or a carrier pigeon. *Something.*"

Kate sighs, rubbing her forehead, and dips her chin in shame. "I'm sorry. You're right. Obviously. I should've called. I'm so, so, sorry," she says, her eyes glistening. "I didn't know what to say. 'Hey, guys, I was kidnapped but I'm okay, and I'm gonna stay with my kidnapper for a little bit longer. That cool?' I mean, what would you have said?"

Honestly? I don't know how to answer her.

My stomach lurches, and I'm embarrassed at how we're taking our frustration out on her instead of the dude who's responsible for this drama. This is Niro's fault, not Kate's. But she defends him and won't tell us the whole story, and that worries me.

"Look, you're home and safe, and we're so fucking grateful for that." Chloe grabs both of Kate's hands and gives them a loving squeeze. "But Varrek is not exactly thrilled to have a scaly blue stranger hanging out in the village. His duty is to protect the clan and you brought a kidnapper home with you. So at some point we'll need actual answers."

"Yeah, I know. You're not mad at me then?" Kate asks.

"Oh, I'm mad as hell," Chloe replies, her gaze finding mine. "You?"

I nod in agreement. "Yeah. My next wrinkle is one hundred percent your fault."

Kate chuckles, and I realize how much I've missed that sound. "I can tell you that Niro did kidnap me," Kate says, "but it was a misunderstanding, honestly. He is a dragon who can shift forms into a humanoid. He can cloak himself to become invisible, which is probably why no one could find me, and he flies in his dragon form. But he has not harassed, assaulted, or raped me."

"Okay, well, that's good, I suppose," Chloe says, skepticism thick in her tone.

I don't want to ask, but I can't stop myself. "Are you… I mean, are you guys, um–"

Kate shakes her head in disgust. "No, nothing has happened between us, if that's what you're thinking. He's pretty, but he's a dick."

I'm thrilled she's not fond of him because that's a good sign he hasn't successfully manipulated her. Kate's an opinionated, spirited little thing with a dark side that frightens many. The longer she despises him and he finds her to be strange and unsettling, which I hope to be the case, the sooner he'll return to his caves and be out of our lives.

"Has anyone in the clan apologized to you yet? For thinking your dragon sightings were bullshit?" Chloe asks.

"Hmm, nope. Nothing yet," Kate replies with a smirk.

"Maybe once the fire-breathing monster leaves the village, they'll come around, ya know?" I add.

Kate stares at her boots, her gaze unfocused, and utters, "Yeah, maybe."

I pull her toward me in a hug. She pretends to push me off, but eventually wraps her arms around me with a giggle. When we both let go, she sighs and says, "Now can we puh-lease talk about your wedding? I need every detail. And whatever you need, I'm here."

* * *

Okay, focus on the breath, Ava. Focus. On. The breath.

I repeat this chant mentally as I breathe in and out while staring at the small hole in my bedroom wall. I practice with my five senses.

Today is my wedding day. A day I didn't think would come ever since I was taken from Earth. But my sweet, sweet lion man has turned my dream into a reality. The day after Kate came home, I told Ahlvo I was ready to start planning the wedding, and to my surprise, he said the planning was basically done and we could have the ceremony in two days. All I had to worry about was what I would wear.

I'm assuming he asked Chloe a ton of questions, because I'm not sure where else he'd learn about human weddings.

I've been trying to tell him about the kid thing since then, but he's been busy either observing training sessions, or discussing what to do about Niro with Varrek and Bruvix. Every night he comes home after I've fallen asleep, and while he usually wakes me up long enough to fool around, we both immediately pass out after.

And… maybe… every time I get the chance, I clam up and my hands shake and I can't get the words out.

I tried having a general discussion on birth control with Kaiva, but I was too much of a chicken to push for an answer on whether their methods would work on humans. Not only is she aware of our upcoming wedding, but she's also Ahlvo's mom, and I'm not sure she'd keep that discussion between us.

Kate is still the only one who knows the truth.

It'll be fine. I'll just tell him after the wedding and before we complete the mating bond, so that way, if he thinks I'm some sort of heartless freak, he still has time to bail on spending his life with me. Which he might.

"Okay, finishing touches, yes?" Chloe says as she strolls in with a handful of delicate yellow flowers.

"Oh, but I already have these," I tell her, showing her the bouquet of wild herbs, weeds, and flowers in various shades of white. It's a rustic arrangement, and it matches my dress perfectly. Well, not *my* dress. It's on loan from Kaiva, and Zohma pinned up the bottom to fit my shorter frame.

"Actually, these are from Ahlvo. He insists you wear them in your hair," Chloe says with an amused look.

"He's turned into quite the groomzilla, hasn't he?" I have no clue why he picked these specifically or why they need to be in my hair, but I trust him and I'm so excited to see his vision of what our wedding should look like.

Chloe stands behind me holding a single flower in one hand and the rest in the other, looking at my hair thoughtfully. "So what are we thinking with these?"

"Maybe we can slip them in like this?" I say, pointing to the shape I have in mind.

"Totally! That will look amazing," she pauses, then before touching my hair, says, "May I?"

I smile. "Yes, you may," I tell her.

I take half of the flowers from her, and we stick the stems into my braids until they start to form a crown.

When we're done, I give Chloe a spin, and she gives me a teary-eyed nod of approval. "You look like a queen, Ava," she says. "Absolutely stunning."

Kate pops her head in through the doorway. "We ready to get this show on th—" she stops mid-sentence, taking me in. "Christ, Ava! You are so beautiful. Ahlvo is going to piss himself when he sees you."

I chuckle at her ability to be vulgar in this moment. "Uh, I really hope you're wrong, but thanks, Red."

Kate and Chloe wear lavender dresses in slightly different styles. One is Nalba's, altered into an empire silhouette to fit Chloe and her small baby bump, and one is Zohma's old halter dress dyed lavender to match and altered to fit Kate's short and voluptuous frame. I had no idea matching bridesmaid dresses were even possible with our limited resources, but, man, Zohma is crafty.

"Oh! I almost forgot, here," Kate says as she hands me a bundle of gold fabric with fringes on the bottom. "It's one of Kaiva's shawls. So now you have something old and something borrowed."

"Aww, I love it," I say, draping it over my shoulders. "But I don't really believe in—"

"Now we just need something blue and something new," Kate interrupts. She pokes the tip of her chin with her pointer finger, lost in thought.

"The bouquet is new!" Chloe exclaims.

"And Niro is here. He could be your something blue," Kate adds.

Chloe narrows her gaze. "But I thought the bride had to wear all of those items?"

"Yeah, and no offense Kate, but I don't consider your kidnapping dragon friend to be an integral part of my nuptials."

Kate nods, unbothered. "Fair enough."

"How did you convince Varrek to let Niro attend the wedding?" I ask.

Kate laughs. "Well, the crew will be seated in a circle around Niro and me for the ceremony, and I'm pretty sure they're all armed to the teeth just in case he tries something. Which he won't! I promise he won't."

"I also played the baby card," Chloe says, rubbing a hand over her belly. "I told Varrek how important it was for the three of us to be together today and just let the hormonal tears take care of the rest."

"Genius," I tell Chloe.

"Ah!" Chloe suddenly shouts, shooting to her feet. "Your something blue! I've got it. Be right back."

She runs out of the room, and I hear her dash out the front door, slamming it shut, and then I hear her slam another door, which I assume is Varrek's, next door. A minute later, Chloe returns, panting heavily, holding a strip of leather that's been dyed a dark blue color.

"What is this?" I ask as she places it in my palm.

"I have no idea. It was in Varrek's weapon room. But I was thinking you could wear it as a garter."

It looks too big for my wrist, so that might be the best option. "Good call."

I pull up my dress and Chloe and Kate bend down to tie it around my thigh. They stand back and look at me expectantly. "Ready?" Kate asks.

I nod. "Ready."

Instead of having them walk before me, I asked them to stand on either side like they're giving me away. And in a way, they are. They're the only human family I have left, and I feel incredibly grateful to have them with me for such an important moment.

Niro leans against the side of our house, and as we pass, he follows, staying several feet back.

The girls and I walk together, their arms linked through mine as I hold the bouquet, along the main path of the village, damp blue moss squishing under our boots.

The ground may be wet, but luckily the air is dry. For now.

Please don't rain. Please don't rain.

The path is lined with douku orbs, and many more hang in the trees above, creating a dimly lit, romantic atmosphere. The evening sky is a rich, dark purple, slightly darker than Ahlvo's eyes. I can see the meal hall where the clan is gathered, and their mussashk harpist is plucking away at the strings, the sounds like a spa.

We arrive at the meal hall, and my eyes meet Ahlvo's. He's bare chested, just how I like. His cane leans against the wall behind him, and his hair is neatly braided. And within those braids are what must be hundreds of the same yellow flowers I have weaved in my hair. The ones he insisted I wear.

He wanted us to match. My heart nearly explodes at the realization.

Ahlvo really went above and beyond what I ever could've expected. The decorations, the lighting—everywhere I look, I see ethereal beauty. Romance. He did this all for me.

My palms start to sweat when I think about all the good things Ahlvo deserves in this life. I wonder if I'm truly worthy of being his mate.

We join him where he stands at the back of the meal hall, the clan seated on the long wooden benches throughout. Chloe starts giggling at my side and leans toward Ahlvo. "Um, when I said we need lots of flowers, I didn't mean *you* had to wear them, Ahlvo."

His face falls, and he touches a flower sticking out from the tip of one of his braids. "Does it look wrong?" he asks.

"No, no, no!" Chloe assures him. "It's just that the bride is usually the one with the flowers."

He blinks at her for a moment, and then gives me a loving gaze, tossing his braid behind him before telling Chloe, "I chose this flower because it reminds me of Aye-vah. Its petals remain open, giving, through sunshine or rain, as it continues to grow to its tallest height. To the peak of its potential. This flower grows throughout all seasons. It is steadfast and strong. Like Aye-vah, it radiates joy."

A sob bubbles up my throat, but I push it down. We're barely started—I can't cry yet. Although, after hearing why he chose this flower, I'm worried my vows are nowhere near as impressive as his. Who knew he was such a poet?

"And you said that we are to look pretty, Cloh-ee," Ahlvo adds with a cocky grin. "Do I not look pretty?"

Chloe's lips quirk up at the corners, and she gives Ahlvo's forearm a squeeze. "My bad, Ahlvo. You're totally right. You look very pretty. Flowers look good on you." She gives him a final pat on the arm before heading to her seat next to Varrek.

Kate approaches Ahlvo next. "You will make her so happy that she shits rainbows, or so help me, I will destroy you."

Ahlvo tilts his head at her, then whispers, "I assure you, rainbows will be shat."

This catches Kate off guard, and she lets out a high-pitched snorting cackle. Before she leaves, she leans in and says, "I heard you worked really hard to find me and bring me home. Just… thank you."

Her seat is a few rows behind Chloe, next to a cranky looking Niro, and one row in front of an even crankier looking Bruvix, whose gaze is shooting daggers at the back of Niro's head. The rest of the clan occasionally glances at Niro, keeping their distance.

I know they're scared, and I don't blame them. I don't want him here either, but I can't pay attention to that right now. I need to marry my mate.

Ahlvo takes my hands in his and clears his throat. "Aye-vah, I do not know much about human weddings or about your species in general. Sometimes I worry about how small your noses are. How do you breathe with those tiny things? But even if humans still seem strange to me, you do not. I have had the honor of learning all of your smiles and what they mean. I know that when your pink tongue sticks out, you are so focused on your task that you would not notice if an asteroid crashed in a ball of fire at your feet."

The clan erupts in laughter, and so do I. It's true.

"And I know that you will care for everyone else before you assess your own needs, which makes you a very stubborn patient, and I will never let you forget that," he adds with a wink.

Then his tone turns more serious. "Despite the losses you have endured, you enter each day with an open mind and an eagerness to help others. I do not know if I will ever deserve your loving heart, but I will spend every moment trying to make your eyes shine bright with happiness."

I sniff my tears back, but they fall anyway. When a snot bubble starts to form, I wipe it away while tears flow down my face in thick streaks. I laugh nervously at how I'm crying too hard to speak, but then my hands begin to shake. I let go of Ahlvo's hands so he doesn't notice, but my silence is going from sweet to awkward pretty quickly, and I have no idea what to do. My breaths get shorter, and concern fills Ahlvo's eyes.

A single bead of sweat rolls down my back, and my scalp suddenly feels itchy. I force a smile at the clan, but even I can tell it looks fake. It certainly feels fake. My belly fills with panic and when I can't stand the quiet anymore, I blurt, "I object!"

CHAPTER 24

AHLVO

I am… confused. Cloh-ee said nothing about objections during the vows, but perhaps the bride must object before reciting hers? And this is a tradition Cloh-ee forgot to tell me?

Immediately after Aye-vah objects to our wedding, she tugs me by the hand until we are behind the meal hall, away from the clan and surrounded by twigs and bushes. She is still crying and breathing erratically, and I am growing increasingly afraid.

"My mate, what is wrong?" I ask, cupping her face in my hands.

"It's, it's…" Aye-vah places her hands around my wrists, pulling my hands from her face. She begins pacing in a small circle. "There's something I haven't told you that I should've told you a long time ago, but I didn't because… Well, at first, I didn't think it mattered. And then I was worried how you would react, and now it's our wedding day and everything is so perfect, and there's no more time, and we have to talk about it *right now*."

"Aye-vah. Aye-vah, please," I plead. "Look at me, little noodle."

She does, and I bend down so I can press my forehead against hers. "Whatever it is you must tell me, say it."

She pulls back so she can hold my gaze. She swallows, still delaying, and I squeeze her shoulders. Finally, she says, "I don't want kids."

I let the words settle in my mind.

"I mean, I don't *think* I want kids. I'm not sure," Aye-vah adds, panicked.

I nod, taking it in. "This means… never?"

"I don't know. Growing up, I always thought having kids was inevitable, you know? My childhood wasn't the best because of my dad, but since my mom was wonderful, I just assumed I would be that kind of mom to my own child. And once I got older, everyone I knew started getting pregnant and having kids. But I kept waiting for that feeling, that… that certainty that would signify I was meant to be a mother. It never came. I think if I had gotten pregnant accidentally, I could've made it work—motherhood, that is. And I think I could be an excellent mom. It's not that I don't like kids. I *love* kids. I love their little fat feet and their sometimes-brutal honesty. How they manage to get food all over their faces and in their hair but not in their mouths."

"Okay…" I trail off, encouraging her to keep talking.

"I'm not saying I'm expecting to ever feel *ready* for motherhood, because I know you never really feel ready. It just happens, and you figure it out as you go." Aye-vah pauses and stops pacing. She sighs long and hard. "But when I dig deep, when I look closely at whether or not being a mom is something I *want* to do… at best, I'm not sure. And at worst, the answer is no."

"No," I repeat quietly.

"I just think this is a big decision. One you can't take back," Aye-vah continues. "And once you become a mom, you're a mom for life. If this is something I'm going to do for the rest of my life, I should at least be certain it's something I want to do. Otherwise, I shouldn't do it."

I think about her words, about becoming a father, and what that future would look like. How it would feel to watch Varrek and Bruvix and the others become fathers around me. I imagine my mother and father holding my newborn child, and how much love that child would receive from them. I think about Aye-vah, her belly heavy with my offspring, and how incredible she would be at caring for a child that looked like me, but hopefully, more like her.

Then I think about the life I lived on Trovilia, the life I lived here on Oluura before meeting Aye-vah, and the joy I have felt since first laying eyes on her. And my words come easily. "Very well, inara. We will not have children."

Aye-vah stares at me for so long that I wonder if she heard me.

"What?" she asks, her tone filled with disbelief. "You're just okay with this? You're not mad or disappointed? Or… or feel like you'll be missing out on fatherhood?"

"Yes, no, and no," I reply simply to each of her questions.

"But what about how your clan is lacking in females? And now we know humans are compatible for procreation. Aren't we expected to have kids if we become mated? Wouldn't it make the clan mad if I decide not to?"

I scoff. "I do not care how the clan feels about our life together. If you do not want children, then I do not want children either. What the clan thinks does not matter."

She purses her lips, still not convinced I am speaking truth. "Aye-vah, I am a warrior from a poor village of Trovilia. I am the only child of a healer and hunter. I never expected to reach an age where I could become a father."

Her eyes widen, so I explain. "Warriors who do not come from wealthy families rarely live long lives. When we die in battle, our name becomes honorable because of our sacrifice, and our families are given enough credits to live comfortably."

"Wow, really?" she asks.

"Yes. That was the future I envisioned for myself. A short life. And then, when our females died from sickness, any hope I had of finding a mate was lost. And then we fled Trovilia and came here where I planned to protect my clan until my last breath.

"I spent most of my life never expecting to find a mate, let alone become a father. Having a child always felt too far beyond my grasp," I tell her.

"Okay, but, Ahlvo," she says, her small hands encircling my wrists. "Now you do have a mate. You were so happy when you talked about all the 'little ones running around the village someday.' And now a child is more possible than you previously thought."

"No, it is not," I reply. "You are my mate, Aye-vah. If having children is not something that would make you happy, then is it not possible for me."

"But—"

"Aye-vah, please listen," I interject. I know what she is doing, and I will not let her. "Your happiness may not matter to you, but it is all that matters to me. And this has not taken me by complete surprise. I noticed your fear scent when we watched Cloh-ee's message. When she told us about the baby, it was thick in my nose. I had a feeling you did not want to follow her path, but I was not certain. I will not do anything to create fear in your heart. I cannot be happy if you are unhappy."

"Really? You're sure?" she asks, her smile wide with hope. Finally, she is starting to believe my words.

"Of course. My love for you is not dependent upon your willingness to become a mother. I will love you until the end of my days no matter what our family looks like. The two of us can be our own family."

Her eyes fill with tears once again, but this time, they are paired with her smile which calms my nerves.

She sniffles and wipes her face. "Okay, let's get married."

We race around to the front of the meal hall and take our places once more before the clan. I hear whispers from several members, and I cannot make out much of what they are saying, but there seems to be a lot of confusion.

"Ava, you didn't need to wait for me to come home in order to object to your own wedding, really," Kay-teh teases.

"Sorry, guys," Aye-vah mutters as she takes my hands in hers. "Little hiccup, but we're good to go now. Great even." Her smile is beautiful. She is relaxed in a way she wasn't when she walked down the aisle.

She straightens her spine, takes a deep breath, and begins with her vows. "Whew, okay. Ahlvo, I don't think I ever knew what real love felt like until I met you. I thought I did, but I was wrong. Real love is better, and more generous than I ever expected. It's about taking care of each other and approaching everything as a team without having to sacrifice parts of yourself to do so. It's empowering, but somehow also selfless. It's friendship and lust and butterflies and trust. It's…better than any fantasy."

I hear multiple sniffles in the crowd, and I look up to see it is my mother and Cloh-ee.

"You, Ahlvo, are my favorite person. You're my best friend. I am so honored to be your inara, and I can't wait to grow old with you." Then she asks, "Do you take me?"

"I do. *In perpetuum et unum diem*," I reply. "Do you take me?"

"I do," she says. "*In perpetuum et unum diem.*"

Then she presses her lips to mine, and I lift her in my arms. The clan cheers, but I barely hear them. My focus is on my inara's small, soft tongue, and how it swirls around mine.

Eventually, our lips separate with a final peck. There will be plenty of time for kisses after the wedding, and for now, we will join the clan for the feast Waldric has prepared.

We celebrate as a clan, surrounded by music and laughter. Bruvix ensures that every mug is filled with his special wedding ale, which is sweeter than his normal, bitter batches, and I like this one quite a bit. I thank him as he refills my glass, but he is too drunk to accept my compliment. I watch as he refills Kay-teh's mug, but when Nee-roh the draxilio lifts his mug for a refill, Bruvix shouts "None for you!" in his face and stomps off.

It seems he is jealous of the time Nee-roh has spent with Kay-teh. I make a mental note of this so I can discuss it with him after Aye-vah and I are mated. I do not have the time nor energy for anything else until then.

I take a sip of ale and notice Aye-vah's eyes on me. I lower my mug to the table and ask, "Do you approve of this?"

"What? You drinking?"

"Yes. Because if you do not want me to drink Bruvix's ale, it would not be a loss to stop," I reply.

She chuckles. "No, no. It's fine. I was nervous before, worried you'd use alcohol to cope or drink while taking your pain medication. But... I think I was just scared."

"Because of your father?" I ask in a quiet voice so no one hears. I do not know how many members of our clan Aye-vah has confided in about her father, but I assume the number is small.

"Yeah," she says, leaning her head against my shoulder. "But you're different. My father never respected my mother. I could tell whenever she tried to bring up his drinking and how she felt that he wasn't really listening. She didn't mention it to him often, but when she did, he dismissed her concern as an overreaction. You've shown me over and over that you respect me. I think you're starting to respect yourself again too. So I trust you to determine what your body can handle, and if I ever grow concerned about that, I know you'll listen."

Once our bellies are full and the clan's inhibitions have been lowered by ale, we spill out onto the main path to dance. My mother and father twirl past us, and my father plucks a flower from my mane and tucks it into one of his own braids. Aye-vah even shows the clan how to do the chih-khen dance. Finally the music slows, and I pull my mate into my arms, pressing her body against mine.

"Are you enjoying your wedding, my mate?" I ask as I trace her small ear with my finger. "Was it how you imagined?"

"Mmm," she moans softly. "Better. It's perfect."

I catch Varrek's eye as he dances with Cloh-ee, and I notice he has added a single yellow flower to his hair as well. Cloh-ee has too. "We wanted to look pretty as well, brother," he hollers, and Aye-vah gives him what she calls a "thumbs-up."

My mate and I hold each other close and sway to the music, and with her scent all over me, I wonder how soon we can retire to our home. They would not notice or blame us for leaving to complete the mating ceremony, but if Aye-vah is having fun, I do not want to pull her away too early.

A heartbeat later, the sky opens up and rain pours through the trees. Most of the clan scatters immediately. Cloh-ee pulls Varrek along by the hand toward their home, holding her other hand above her head.

Kay-teh and Nee-roh stand close together, not touching, and look up at the falling rain with matching smiles.

Bruvix sits on the one bench not protected by the roof of the meal hall, unbothered, and continues to drink his ale as rain splashes into his mug, glaring occasionally at Nee-roh. Nalba, in true Nalba fashion, stumbles toward her shop with a full mug in hand. Waldric offers her a hand as she passes by, and instead of taking it, Nalba sloppily throws herself into his arms.

The Hexrins continue to dance in a tight circle despite the lack of music, as the musicians were the first to flee the rain.

I should probably have someone ensure that Nee-roh returns to his quarters in the small storage shed behind the meal hall, and that Kay-teh makes her way to my old room above my mother's med room, but I am far too distracted. The way my mate's wet dress clings to her hips…

I expect Aye-vah to race toward our home—as she is not fond of the rain—but she does not. She remains in place, looking up at me with that brilliant smile of hers, and chuckles as large raindrops fall into her open palms. In this moment, it is clear she is truly present, here to appreciate the life we are about to begin. Rain and all.

With my cane in one hand, I wrap my other hand around the back of her neck and bring her lips toward mine. I kiss her, long and deep, and Aye-vah's arms wrap around my neck, pulling me closer. "Make me yours," she says against my lips, her voice husky.

My chest rumbles with a steady growl at the feel of our soaked bodies pressed against each other. I stride as fast as my leg will allow, pulling Aye-vah by the hand, and throw the door closed behind us once we enter our home. Finally we're alone. I take the steps two at a time, pulling Aye-vah along behind me, the muscles in my leg screaming at the pressure I am putting on it. But I care not because nothing will stop me from taking my mate and marking her neck with my bite.

"Ahlvo. I need you now," she moans against my palm before pressing her lips against it. We make it to the second floor, which is Kay-teh's old room, and Aye-vah pulls me around to face her. "Here.

Right fucking here," she breathes as she starts pawing at the waistband of my pants.

"Wait, are there any human wedding traditions I am forgetting to honor?" I ask as my pants fall to the floor around my ankles. I kick off my boots and step out of my pants as Aye-vah presses her back against the wall. Her chest is heaving, her nipples are pebbled beneath her dress, and I trace the outline through the soaked, nearly translucent fabric. When I pinch her nipple between my fingers, she sucks in a breath and releases a whimper.

"I–I'm wearing a garter on my thigh," she mutters low. "You're supposed to remove it with your teeth."

What a delightful custom. It is like a treasure hunt.

I shoot my mate a wicked grin as I fall to my knees before her and slowly lift the hem of her dress. I remove her boots, one at a time, and press a kiss to each ankle. I take my time, peppering her shin, calf, and then knee with kisses. My tongue flicks as I lift her dress higher. Aye-vah cries out, and her hands slam against the wall behind her. When her delicious, wide thighs are exposed, I find the item she mentioned, and I freeze in place.

"Aye-vah, where did you get this?" I ask, trying to conceal the alarm and jealousy in my tone.

She glances down, and shrugs, confusion swirling in her eyes. "Oh, Chloe gave it to me. I think it's Varrek's or something."

It is indeed Varrek's, and Aye-vah should not be wearing it.

"Hey, what's wrong?" Aye-vah asks as she lifts my chin.

"This is a wristband Varrek was awarded when he became leader of the Trovilian warriors," I tell her.

She tilts her head and narrows her gaze. "Am I missing something? Tell me why this is such a big no-no."

"It is something that Varrek cherishes, so I do not think he would be happy knowing I removed it from your thigh with my teeth. But more importantly, anything you place on your body, specifically my favorite parts of your body, should not belong to anyone but me."

Aye-vah purses her lips, trying to hide a grin. "I should probably put my foot down and tell you that jealousy isn't a good look, but... I kinda love this possessive side of you. As long as it doesn't get out of control," she amends.

Then she leans down and unties the band from her thigh, tossing it across the room onto Kay-teh's bed. "It was just something blue that Chloe let me borrow. I didn't choose it because it's Varrek's. I'm yours, lion man. Now are you going to eat my pussy or what?"

Demanding little thing. I am incredibly proud to be hers.

"Is that what you want?" I ask, brushing her hands away and letting my breath fan her thighs. "You want my tongue on your pretty cunt?"

She closes her eyes and leans her head against the wall. "Yes. Please."

I reach up to her ribs and tug on the strings holding her dress in place. It falls open at the front, and she shimmies her shoulders out until the dress lands in a pile between her feet and the wall behind her.

Then my tongue is on her. I part her glistening, swollen folds and lap at her center. She is already so wet for me, and yet I will never get enough of her taste. I try to take my time, savoring her, but the tether is shattering my control. I am desperate to claim her. I have waited far too long to make her mine. Her hands find my mane, and she pulls hard. A groan slips from my throat as I flick my tongue at her clit, stroking it rapidly.

"Yes, yes, yes, yessssss," Aye-vah pants.

I toss her legs over my shoulders and use the wall to slide her body upward as I stand. She shrieks in surprise, but I steady her, holding her, licking her. She continues to mewl, thrashing her head side to side. Yellow petals fall from her hair with each jerk of her neck, and it is as if the goddess is blessing our mating by showering us with flowers.

Aye-vah's thighs clutch my head and start to shake, and I pick up the pace, determined to make this orgasm one she shall never forget. I let my fang graze her clit as I fuck her with my tongue, showing her what I plan to do with my cock very soon. She screams my name, followed by many sounds and words I cannot identify as her walls close in around my tongue, squeezing me like a vise, but I do not stop or slow my pace. I continue lapping up her sweet juices and trace her folds with my tongue.

When the quaking of her body ceases, I pull away, licking my lips as I slide her body down the wall, positioning her core right where I need it. She throws her arms around my neck and holds on tightly. "Don't drop me," she whispers.

"Never," I vow.

She reaches a hand between us and guides my cock inside her center slowly. I slide into her easily, and once I reach halfway, I push forward until we're hip to hip. She gasps and her lips crash onto mine. She moans against my lips and murmurs, "I can taste myself."

"Delicious one, you are," I reply, and she giggles softly as her tongue swipes against my lips.

I pull out slowly, almost all the way, and then slam back into her heat. I create a steady rhythm, and she grunts against my mouth as my cock begins to vibrate inside her. The wall behind her creaks each time I pound into her. Her thighs shiver, and I know she is close. I break our kiss as my fangs extend, and kissing a trail from her jaw to her shoulder, I ready myself for the mating bite.

"Ohhh, Ahlvo, yes! I'm coming!" she shouts as I sink my fangs into the spot where her neck and shoulder meet. Her screams get louder, and I hope the pleasure covers the pain. Her blood covers my tongue, and I drink it down. Her cunt spasms around my cock, and I have never felt such ecstasy. I press my tongue against the wound, cleaning and kissing her mark as she continues to dig her blunt claws into my scalp.

Just as she begins to come down, I feel my sac tighten, and I slam my cock into her as my fingers dig into the fleshy globes of her ass. "You must bite me, Aye-vah," I command. She brushes my braids behind my neck on one side and sinks her square teeth into my flesh. The feeling of her breaking my skin, of sealing our bond, as I remain deep inside her obliterates any remaining control I have, and within one beat of my heart, I look to the sky and roar. I spill into her. I am frozen in pleasure and never want to leave this feeling.

Aye-vah's smooth tongue glides against the mark she made as I hold her against the wall, panting into her mussed mane.

Refusing to leave her body, I push away from the wall and carry her up another level until we reach our room. There is very little time before we will fall into a deep sleep and solidify the mental link between us. My leg aches from the strenuous activity, but I do not regret it in the slightest. I welcome the pain.

I drop Aye-vah's lush body on top of the furs, and she releases a whimper when I pull out of her. "I shall be back, inara," I tell her then grab a towel and clean her thighs.

I do the same for myself and toss the towel aside before climbing into our bed and wrapping my body around hers from behind.

Aye-vah lets out a yawn, and I press a kiss to her hair. "Oh shit," she says.

"What is it?"

"You didn't pull out," she says, worry thick in her voice. "I'm not ovulating, but still…"

"We shall be more careful next time. Do not worry." I caress her shoulder, trying to comfort her. Soon enough, I will be better equipped to ease my mate's fears as I will be inside her mind, and I am very much looking forward to that.

She yawns again, and I watch her eyelids getting heavier by the moment. "I'll talk to Kaiva about birth control tomorrow," she mumbles, cuddling deeper into the pillows and blankets around us. Her breathing evens, and I hear a delicate snore muffled by the pillow pressed against her face.

"All will be well. Always," I whisper against her neck, letting sleep pull me under along with her.

EPILOGUE

AVA

*Y*ou *cheat. You do not play fair,* Ahlvo sends me as he continues working on my hair. I'm seated in front of him on our bed and his fingers are swift and gentle as he pulls my hair into tight twists.

How could I cheat? It isn't a thinking game. Hand Slap is all about speed, I send back. *Just admit I'm better than you.*

Never! he protests.

It's been three days since our wedding, and as many times as we've had sex since, we've played the Hand Slap Game. Ahlvo is obsessed with it. Probably because I keep beating him.

Okay, I am finished. He sends as his hands leave my hair.

I reach back and run my fingers along my twists, inspecting his work. *Well done, my love.*

He wraps his arms around me as I lean my head back against his hard chest. *Yes, I have many, many talents.*

I laugh, threading my fingers through his. *This is true.*

He traces a line up my arm with a finger and stops when he reaches the thin gold band around my bicep. *Are you sure this is not uncomfortable to wear?* he sends.

No, I don't even notice it, I tell him, silently thanking the goddess that Trovilian birth control is safe for humans to use, especially since it's in the form of jewelry.

I am glad you are relieved. I told you my mother would have a solution and would not judge you.

You were right. You're quite wise, you know, I send back. *But we really should've been more careful.*

He leans down and kisses my cheek. *It was a close call, but you are not pregnant and there is nothing to worry about.*

I nod.

I recall seeing mated women on Trovilia wearing these. We are not the first mated couple to not want kids.

Kaiva told me the same thing, but it's still comforting to hear it again.

He holds me closer, even though I'm as close as I can get.

I am certain we can be closer than this, inara, he sends along with several images of him fucking me against the wall on our wedding night.

My cheeks flush, and I feel myself getting wet already.

Mmm, do you need me, Ava? he asks, the usual pause in my name is removed through our mental link.

Say it again, I demand.

Your name? Ava. Ava, Ava, Ava.

I smile, loving the new way my name sounds through our mental link. It's not like he said it incorrectly before, there was just a long pause in the middle. I like it that way too, but I also love it this way.

I look out the window, noting the dreary skies and the drizzling rain. *I should get going. Chloe is starting to get bigger, and I promised I'd be there when Kaiva does her sonogram. We aren't sure how long her gestation period will be, but since pregnancy for your people is six moon cycles and ours is nine, we think Chloe's will be somewhere in between.*

Ahlvo grumbles, pressing a loud smacking kiss to my temple. *I should go as well. I need to practice some new maneuvers with the cane.*

I feel his motivation pulsing through my head and see the stances he plans to start from, first with the cane, and then with the sword. I see them transform into the swift movements he will use on an attacker. They are fast and graceful, and I couldn't be prouder of him.

It is all because of you, he sends, reading my thoughts.

Hey! You peeped! Don't peep on my brain.

I do not know how not to peep, I am afraid, he replies with a chuckle.

Okay, but you need to try really hard not to because about an hour before lunch I have my first session with Varrek.

For ther-ah-pee? he asks. *What does Varrek wish to discuss?*

I'm not sure. Chloe just said he was interested in trying it out. And I couldn't tell you even if I knew! That's confidential.

Yes, yes, I understand, he sends. *But how can I remain out of your head for an entire hour? I suppose I could run some training drills…*

No, I don't want you to push yourself too hard. You just became Varrek's second-in-command again; I don't want you to hurt yourself, I reply.

What if the angry fog returns? he asks.

Do what we've practiced, the 5-4-3-2-1 method using your senses, I tell him. *I've seen the angry fog in action, and I'm not a fan. And if it's still spewing bullshit lies about your abilities when my session with Varrek is over, I'm happy to rip it a new asshole.*

It still shows up occasionally, and I'm sure that will continue. But as long as I can help Ahlvo get out of his head or at least scream over the fog about how wonderful and kind Ahlvo is, I know he'll be okay. I've also seen him complete the meditation method by envisioning himself slashing through the red fog with his new cane sword, an image that leaves him feeling confident. He'll fight for himself; I know that now.

Then a brilliant idea pops into my head: *Oh! Think about my ass.*

Instantly, I'm hit with an onslaught of images of my ass. My ass jiggling as I walk away from him, my ass shaking when I danced with him at Maevstra, my ass bouncing when we tried reverse cowgirl last night…

That'll do it.

We get dressed, then he follows me down the stairs and out the front door. I pull the hood of my cloak over my hair, shielding me from the rain. Ahlvo is bare-chested and striding confidently down the path as if it's a lovely sunny day.

When we reach Kaiva's, he pulls me in for a deep, toe-curling kiss. The kiss ends, leaving me dazed as Ahlvo shoots me a cocky grin and walks away. Cane in hand, he moves in the direction of the training grounds.

I head inside and remove my cloak.

"Ava!" Chloe exclaims from the med tube. She's sitting inside with the cover pulled back. Kaiva is at the head of the tube, and Varrek hovers next to Chloe, looking anxious.

"All right, it's baby time!" I say as I clasp my hands together happily.

How much longer until I can see my mate? Ahlvo sends with an image of him frowning. I chuckle and everyone gives me a strange look.

Then recognition fills Chloe's gaze. "Ah, chatting with Ahlvo?"

"Maybe," I reply sheepishly.

You just saw me, I send back.

O fah, I do not care. I miss you already.

My sweet mate. I'm so lucky.

No. I am the lucky one, he argues.

No. I am! I send back.

He sends me a growl. *I. Am.*

Ugh, we are gross, I send with an eye roll. *We could go on like this all day.*

And we shall. In perpetuum et unum diem, inara.

My heart skips. In perpetuum et unum diem *indeed.*

* * *

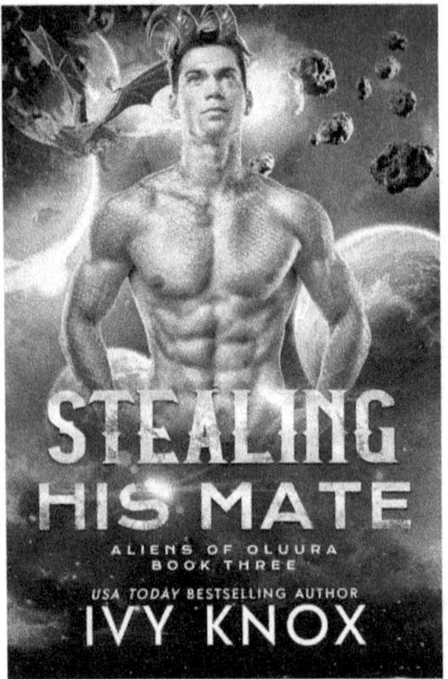

Thank you for reading CHARMING HIS MATE! I hope you loved Ava and Ahlvo's story. I know what you're thinking…what the heck happened to Kate? And who is this Niro guy she brought back with her? What's his deal? Well, now's your chance to find out.

STEALING HIS MATE is available now!

"Another magnificent addition to the series. It's filled with mysteries, danger, drama, adventure, steamy romance and wonderful characters. I couldn't put it down and cannot wait to see what happens next!" - 5-star reader review

Kate has had enough. She's sick of getting dirty looks from the clan, sick of being seen as the village weirdo, and sick of existing on this strange planet. Meanwhile, her best friends are getting married and pregnant and settling into their happily ever afters, leaving Kate with too much free time and no one to talk to.

A mysterious male with washboard abs and sparkly blue scales keeps appearing in her dreams, jolting her awake, and she has no idea why.

Kidnapped late one night, Kate finally comes face to face with Niro, her dream guy, and she thinks her problems will soon be solved. If they can break this bewildering curse, they can return to their lives, and hopefully, she'll get some sleep.

As they embark on a quest for answers about their dream link that takes them all over Oluura, their lives intertwine in ways they never could've imagined. Each moment, they are tempted to claw each other's eyes out while resisting the urge to rip each other's clothes off.

Can they put their differences aside and break the curse? Or are they destined to crash each other's dreams for the rest of time?

Want to find out what happens next? Start reading Stealing His Mate now!

ALSO FROM IVY

<u>ALIENS OF OLUURA</u>

Saving His Mate

Charming His Mate

Stealing His Mate

Keeping His Mate

Healing His Mate

Enchanting Her Mate

(This series isn't finished. There's plenty more to come!)

<u>STRANDED ON EARTH</u>

Her Alien Bodyguard

Her Alien Neighbor

Her Alien Librarian

Her Alien Student

Her Alien Boss

ENJOY THIS BOOK?

If you liked this book, please leave a review. It helps others find my work. Thank you for reading.

Stay up-to-date on bonus chapters, new releases, cover reveals, giveaways, and general smutty shenanigans by subscribing to my newsletter.

FROM IVY

Let's get right into it, shall we?

Ava and Ahlvo are both brilliant, selfless, and incredibly stubborn. I adore them.

I knew the moment I introduced charming Ahlvo that his love story would begin with him in a dark place. Otherwise, it would be impossible for Ava to resist him. There would be no hesitation for Ava. And if he weren't haunted by "the angry fog," aka the voice of his depression, he would've pursued Ava relentlessly until she fell for him. Plus, I'm a big fan of the friends-to-lovers trope and wanted to see how that would play out for these two.

Getting them away from the rest of the clan opened up all kinds of opportunities for heated glances and charged moments. While the clan does not see sex as a taboo subject like us humans, it still would've been hard/weird for Ahlvo to try to woo Ava with his mom constantly around, ya know?

As for Ava, I wanted her to find a way to walk the line between holding space for Ahlvo's pain and taking on the entirety of his emotional burden as her own. I've often wondered how empathetic people who become therapists can master this skill because it must be so difficult, and Ava is determined to maintain healthy boundaries while also being there for him.

I hope you enjoyed their push and pull as much as I enjoyed writing it!

Now, let's talk about Kate.

Many of you have mentioned how excited you are for her story and to learn more about the blue dragon. Well, that time has come! Kate's book is up next, and you'll get to know all about Niro and how Bruvix feels about Kate's new friend. GET EXCITED!

Love,
	Ivy

P.S. Endless thanks and hugs to my editor, Tina, who helped me give this story the makeover it needed, my sensitivity reader, Grace, who helped me honor Ava and her background, my beta readers, and my other editor, Mandi, who gave me brilliant notes on how to elevate the most crucial scenes in this story. It takes a village, as they say, and my village has the very best people in it.

RESOURCES

SAMHSA (Substance Abuse and Mental Health Services
Administration Hotline)
1-800-662-HELP (4357)
TTY: 1-800-487-4889
samhsa.gov

National Suicide Prevention Hotline
1-800-273-8255 (call or chat)
suicideprevention.org

National Domestic Violence Hotline
1-800-799-SAFE (7233) (call or chat)
thehotline.org

ABOUT IVY

Ivy Knox has always been a voracious reader of romance novels, but quickly found her home in sci-fi romance because, frankly, life on Earth can be kind of a drag. When she's not lost on faraway worlds created by her favorite authors, she's creating her own.

Ivy lives with her husband and two neurotic (but very cute) dogs in the Midwest. When she's not reading or writing, she's probably watching *Superstore, New Girl, What We Do in the Shadows,* or *Fall of the House of Usher* for the millionth time.